The Kennedy Plan

A play

J. A. Jensen

For the 60 million who perished

The Kennedy Plan

Act 1

Scene 1

JOSEPH KENNEDY swings a golf club while his sons JOE JUNIOR and JACK look on. They wait to tee off at a country club in Florida in 1937.

JOE KENNEDY: I guess I'd take Treasury if the boss offered it, but I don't think Henry Morgenthau is ready to retire.

JOE JUNIOR: Do you think we'd be in this recession if you had Morgenthau's job?

JOE KENNEDY: Can't know things like that, Joe, but I believe that I bring some unique skills to the Roosevelt team. I've been sizing up people and making deals for my entire business career.

JACK: They say that politics is more than business, Pop. Businessmen must know when to make deals, and politicians must know when to make wars.

JOE KENNEDY: That's right, Jack. Candidates start off saying that they will never take the country into war and then they become commander-in-chief and, first thing you know, they decide to wave the flag and send all the young men into battle.

JOE JUNIOR: Sometimes wars are necessary.

JOE KENNEDY: That so? Are you sure about that?

JOE JUNIOR: When there are principles involved---

JOE KENNEDY: ---when there are principles involved! Right. You boys should be skeptical when you hear politicians talk about principles. War is a failure of government and of politicians. It should never be regarded as a moment of glory. Keep in mind that I ran a cadet unit at Boston Latin. We had starched uniforms and shined shoes and even gave each other little ribbons for participation.

JACK: You commanded a cadet corps?

JOE KENNEDY: It was in high school, but all those marches and salutes translate into something very powerful. When President Wilson decided to make the world safe for British trade, those men picked up rifles and went to war. Some of them didn't come back.

JOE JUNIOR: Safe for British trade? Isn't that a little cynical, Pop?

JOE KENNEDY: Not cynical enough. In 1916, Wilson ran for re-election on the slogan that "he kept us out of war," but by 1917, he decided that principle demanded that Americans fight.

JACK: Are you're saying that we shouldn't have wars.

JOE KENNEDY: That's it, Jack. I say no more war. I say make deals and make money and the world will become a little better in the process. Almost any peace is better than a war.

JOE JUNIOR: If Treasury is out, what would you take?

JOE KENNEDY: I'd take the job in London. That would put me right in the middle of the action.   No one celebrates the diplomats who keep the armies apart, but they should: preventing a war is much better than winning one.

JACK: The Boston Sunday Post said that you might run for president in 1940.

JOE KENNEDY: Depends on what the President does, Jack. This is his second term—no president has ever run for a third.   If Roosevelt doesn't run, it would be a hard opportunity to turn down.

Scene 2

President FRANKLIN ROOSEVELT sits in the White House with his son JAMES and Secretary of the Treasury, HENRY MORGENTHAU, JR.

JAMES ROOSEVELT: You should put him somewhere, Father. He was on the campaign train in '32 and was more than generous in the '36 election, as well.

ROOSEVELT: Yes, I know, and he's become a major figure since coming to Washington. I must say he's done a great job with the SEC and now with the Maritime Commission, but like every aggressive businessman, he wants a bigger job.

JAMES ROOSEVELT: (to Henry Morgenthau) With the market crash--

HENRY MORGENTHAU: --not really a crash like '29--

ROOSEVELT: --more of crash than we wanted going into the midterms next year--

JAMES ROOSEVELT: --Kennedy thinks that if he had been at Treasury, he'd be able to manage the economy better.

HENRY MORGENTHAU: That's ridiculous.   Every businessman thinks he can manage the economy. There's more to this job than picking stocks.

ROOSEVELT: Joe knows he can't have Treasury, Henry. I've told him that.

JAMES ROOSEVELT: I had a drink with him last week. He says that if we don't want his help on the business side, and he thinks the business side would be a natural fit for him, he is willing to go to London as the Ambassador.

ROOSEVELT: (laughing with Henry Morgenthau) As Ambassador! That's ridiculous! Joe Kennedy working as a diplomat? Did you hear what he did to those sailors down in Uruguay?

HENRY MORGENTHAU: When he invoked the "Mutiny Statute?"

ROOSEVELT: Yes. He told them that because they were on a government ship, they were working for him. Had 14 of them arrested. The unions are still angry as hell. Kennedy criticized Frances Perkins about it.

HENRY MORGENTHAU: Well, that's the point, isn't it, Mr. President? Joe Kennedy is an excellent businessman, but we can't control him, can we?

JAMES ROOSEVELT: Oh, there's no controlling Joe Kennedy, but maybe we need someone like that in London right now.

ROOSEVELT: How so, Son?

JAMES ROOSEVELT: There are so many forces clashing in Europe. Those Nazi bastards stages big rallies and Mussolini pushes his way around. Might be we need someone there to find consensus. Joe is impatient, but he has a good ear for issues and he has made a living finding agreements.

ROOSEVELT: I can't send an Irish Catholic to the Court of St. James. The English have been fighting the Irish for as long as the Germans have been fighting the Slavs. This isn't a good time to stir up trouble.

HENRY MORGENTHAU: We shouldn't hold his religion against him, Mr. President. I'm sure that the Irish Catholics would like to see one of their own in the highest post in England.

JAMES ROOSEVELT: That's right and we can't have an administration of just WASPs and Jews. Our enemies already refer to us as the "Jew Deal."

HENRY MORGENTHAU: There will always be bigotry.

ROOSEVELT: Well, maybe we should put an Irish Catholic in London. Maybe it would send a message that we are a country where achievement matters more than ethnicity. That could go a long way with Herr Hitler talking about pure blood lines.

HENRY MORGENTHAU: He seems like a dangerous man to put in London, Mr. President. Just last week he was criticizing our cuts in the spending programs. Thinks it led to the downturn.

ROOSEVELT: Might be something to that. I think the point is that we need to put him somewhere, Henry. I don't want him sitting with us during cabinet meetings. He thinks he should be in charge.

JAMES ROOSEVELT: He won't criticize us if we're all on the same team. Let's let him mingle at the parties in London. If he thinks he's working for us, if we look bad, he looks bad-- and it will keep him off the front pages all the time.

ROOSEVELT: All right. He can go to London. I hope he can keep that temper of his under control.

Scene 3

Kennedy home in Brookline in February 1938. ROSE KENNEDY and most of her children are dressed for church. Jack wears his bathrobe.

JOE JUNIOR: You are a boy but that doesn't mean you get to throw the ball around in the house. If your sister tells you not to throw it, you show some respect.

13

BOBBY: She's a girl!

JOE JUNIOR: She's your older sister and you will respect her. Tell me that you understand that.

BOBBY: I understand.

JOE JUNIOR: (to all of the assembled children) Papa's going to be the Ambassador to England. We all need to shape up and not embarrass him.

BOBBY: I'm not going to London.

JOE JUNIOR: Yes, you are going and you are going to act like a Kennedy and not throw balls inside the embassy. I'm depending on you to make Papa proud.

Rose Kennedy enters dressed in her Sunday clothes.

ROSE: Is everyone ready for church?

JACK: My stomach's acting up, Mother.

ROSE: Only you know how you feel, Jack. Is your father off the telephone?

Wearing a three-piece suit with his hair neatly combed, Joseph Kennedy enters and is embraced by his children, young and old.

JOE KENNEDY: How is my team? Joe, you look like a million bucks!

JOE JUNIOR: Got some big shoes to fill.

JOE KENNEDY: Wish you could come to London with your mother and me.

JOE JUNIOR: I'll be there as soon as the school year ends.

JOE KENNEDY: We're going to have some fun! Bobby's going to meet the King of England, aren't you, son?

BOBBY smiles.

JOE KENNEDY: Now everyone is going to have to look and act like we are one of the best families in America. Can't have anyone embarrassing us, can we?

Children: No.

JOE KENNEDY: Do you children realize that we will be the first Irish Catholic family to ever serve the United States in London? All the other ambassadors have been from old Protestant families.

JOE JUNIOR: I read that five ambassadors to the Court of St. James went on to become President of the United States.

JOE KENNEDY: That's right, Joe, but I have no political ambitions for myself. I'm only doing this for you children. By my serving as Ambassador to England, the Kennedy family will be ranked among the best families in America and you boys will have big careers-- careers in politics if you play your cards right.

ROSE: That's not the only thing, Joe. Let's remember that serving our country is important, but nothing is as important as serving God. Now, let's get to church before we are late.

ROSEMARY, a slightly heavy woman in her early 20's, pulls her arm away from a large woman who follows her.

ROSEMARY: I can come to church with you, can't I Mother?

ROSE: Of course, dear. But you must be quiet during the sermon.

ROSEMARY: (loudly) I do remain quiet and I don't want her pulling on my arm.

JOE KENNEDY: Will you sit with your brother Joe during the service, Rosemary?

ROSEMARY: I will but he can't hush me.

Rose looks at Joe and Joe Junior

ROSE: We must be respectful of other families, dear.

ROSEMARY: (loudly) I am respectful!

JOE KENNEDY: Jack, are you feeling better?

JACK: Not today, Papa.

JOE KENNEDY: Feel better, son. We want you with us.

JACK: I will.

JOE KENNEDY: Bobby, help me get these girls organized and loaded into the cars.

Bobby stands tall and walks behind his father as they leave for church.

Scene 4

Joseph Kennedy shakes the hand of Rabbi STEPHEN WISE in the American Embassy in London as his first official appointment gets underway in March 1938.

JOE KENNEDY: I'm just getting started, Rabbi Wise. The truth is, you are my first appointment.

RABBI WISE: I'm sure you know that the German Reich Chancellor has pushed through the Nuremberg laws-- laws which revoke citizenship rights for German Jews.

JOE KENNEDY: That fellow Hitler is just a crazy bastard-- there's no getting around that.

RABBI WISE: Now things are becoming much worse for Jews living in Germany.

JOE KENNEDY: I've heard.

RABBI WISE: It hasn't been widely publicized but German Jews are being assaulted in their own country. Jews who fought for the

German side in the Great War are being marginalized, threatened, and in some cases beaten.

JOE KENNEDY: It's a damn outrage.

RABBI WISE: It is an excellent time to facilitate immigration of the Jews to Palestine. The British agreed to support a Jewish Homeland in Palestine in 1917 but now they are starting to waffle on their commitment.

JOE KENNEDY: That I didn't know.

RABBI WISE: The Balfour Declaration promised the world's Jews a return to their ancient homeland. President Roosevelt recognizes how important this is to American Jews as well as Jews throughout the world.

JOE KENNEDY: I'm here as President Roosevelt's personal representative and you can be sure that I will do everything in my power to represent the best interests of the American people.

RABBI WISE: I'm so happy to hear you say that, Ambassador Kennedy. I will tell Felix Frankfurter how supportive you are. I've been meeting in London with British Zionists and we have concluded that American help is critical to the future of Zionism.

JOE KENNEDY: What makes you think that the British are not committed?

RABBI WISE: The Jews have been persecuted for so long, Mr. Kennedy, that it has become necessary for us to develop networks for information.

JOE KENNEDY: I'll find out what I can, Rabbi Wise, and communicate with Secretary of State Hull.

RABBI WISE: Communicate with the President, Mr. Kennedy. Leave the Secretary out of it.

JOE KENNEDY: You say leave the Secretary out of the loop?

RABBI WISE: We have great confidence in our relationship with Mr. Roosevelt.

JOE KENNEDY: Very good, then. I'll communicate on this matter at the highest levels. (Kennedy rises to show Rabbi Wise out.) Let me ask you a question.

RABBI WISE: Of course.

JOE KENNEDY: Do you see all the Jews of Germany wanting to move to Palestine? I mean, I wonder if saying that they should move might put pressure on some who might not want to leave. I'm not sure I'd like to move back to Ireland right now and I think the place is beautiful.

RABBI WISE: We want them to have the choice.

JOE KENNEDY: Right. That makes sense, but what if the economy of Germany suffers as the Jews leave? Might the Nazis decide that they can't afford to lose all those Jewish businesses?

RABBI WISE: Possibly. Maybe the Germans will see that they are making a mistake but with that criminal Hitler in charge, and the fact that he has suspended elections, we need to make sure we have an alternative.

JOE KENNEDY: I'll be talking with the British leadership soon and be able to learn much more.

Scene 5

Ambassador Kennedy, Prime Minister NEVILLE CHAMBERLAIN, and Foreign Secretary Lord HALIFAX meet in the Prime Minister's office.

CHAMBERLAIN: We don't have much time to get acquainted, Mr. Kennedy. You have come at a time of significant tension for His Majesty's Government.

JOE KENNEDY: I have heard that before you entered politics you were a businessman, Mr. Prime Minister.

CHAMBERLAIN: That's true.

JOE KENNEDY: I have some experience in business myself.

HALIFAX: So we have heard, but we are facing some problems here which are going to require the best of our diplomatic skills.

JOE KENNEDY: What is so urgent?

HALIFAX: We believe that Herr Hitler will soon demand annexation with Austria. The Austrian president has offered to have a special election to determine if the Austrians want a union with Germany, but Hitler doesn't like democratic processes.

CHAMBERLAIN: You see, Mr. Kennedy, the tensions with Germany are not new.

JOE KENNEDY: Is that so?

CHAMBERLAIN: At the end of the last war, some members of this government wanted to punish Germany-- not simply accept the tragedy of it all, but wanted to assign blame. The Germans had surrendered based on President Wilson's 14 points-- they thought that the idea of "self-determination" for all nations sounded like a noble agreement for the future-- but that's not the way things turned out.

JOE KENNEDY: They signed the treaty.

CHAMBERLAIN: They did but they didn't want to. The Treaty of Versailles was too much, I'm afraid. We let our most militant people insist that we continue the blockade we had around Germany. The Germans were starved into signing the treaty-- starved after they had surrendered on the basis of the 14 points. The terms of the Treaty were so unreasonable that they insured that someone like Hitler would eventually rise.

JOE KENNEDY: I imagine there is disagreement on that point.

CHAMBERLAIN: The Germans sued for peace before the Americans ever entered the war. They proposed a return to peaceful conditions with no territorial adjustments-- it was an acknowledgement that the whole enterprise was madness.

HALIFAX: Which it most certainly was.

CHAMBERLAIN: Rather than make the peace, the government got the Americans into the war and a harsh and punitive peace was imposed upon the Germans. We could have changed the terms of the peace after it became obvious that it would be impossible for the Germans to meet the treaty obligations.

HALIFAX: We should have modified it ten years ago.

CHAMBERLAIN: The Germans are no longer saying they want peace. They are saying that they were sold out-- stabbed in the back by some of their own people.

HALIFAX: We are trying to avoid another war-- that is our most important goal.

JOE KENNEDY: President Roosevelt told me to express his hope that war be avoided at almost any cost. I need to tell you how adverse Americans are to participate in another European war.

CHAMBERLAIN: Of course.

JOE KENNEDY: Sentiment has never been stronger in the United States against further intervention in Europe. The Congress has passed two Neutrality Acts. So, the President wants me to tell you that if a war does break out, the United States will not be able back you up-- whether you are right or wrong, just or unjust-- there simply isn't support in the United States for another European war.

HALIFAX: That's what we are trying to prevent, but we must defend the Realm.

CHAMBERLAIN: It doesn't help that the German Chancellor has not had the benefit of a formal education or even foreign travel.

HALIFAX: He's more of a gangster, I'm afraid, a gangster in a uniform--

CHAMBERLAIN: -- a gangster in a uniform who has secretly rearmed. When he announced that the Treaty of Versailles was voided, the western powers should have rearmed.

HALIFAX: That's our biggest problem. The pacifists in England believe that if weapons are not made, they can't be used. They reason that the best way to avoid war is to avoid making guns.

CHAMBERLAIN: That was an ill-considered notion, in retrospect. We don't have anything close to the air power that Herr Hitler now directs.

HALIFAX: We need to build planes and tanks and we will if given the necessary time.

CHAMBERLAIN: Our most important goal is to avoid war. The British Empire is not without any defenses-- we are not as strong as we should be-- but we can defend ourselves here. Rather than shoot bullets and kill the innocent, as always happens in wars, we choose to work with Hitler, as unpleasant as he is.

Scene 6

Ambassador Joseph Kennedy and his wife Rose attend a party with British royalty and high society.

DIPLOMAT: Lady Astor, this is United States Ambassador Joseph Kennedy and Mrs. Kennedy.

LADY ASTOR: Your Excellency...

JOE KENNEDY: Lady Astor, it is a great pleasure to meet you.

LADY ASTOR: Are you enjoying yourself in London, Mrs. Kennedy?

ROSE: We're thrilled to be here. Everyone has been kind and welcoming. We've been to many formal dinners as well as regattas and Scottish hunting parties. We are having a wonderful time!

LADY ASTOR: Have you met the King and Queen.

ROSE: We have. My daughters Rosemary and Katherine-- we call her Kick-- were presented at court.

LADY ASTOR: I've heard such wonderful things about Kick. She's taken London by storm. Rosemary is the one who has more difficulties.

ROSE: That's right. Rosemary does the best she can.

JOE KENNEDY: I can hear your Virginia accent, Lady Astor.

ROSE: We understand you were the first woman in the Parliament.

LADY ASTOR: I was the first woman to be seated, but I started in Virginia.

JOE KENNEDY: Prime Minister Chamberlain told me that you've been supportive of his ideas about trying to deal with the Nazi government in Germany.

LADY ASTOR: It's hard for me to understand why some folks are so intent on stirring up trouble. If we don't find a way to get along with Mr. Hitler, we're going to end up in another war, but there are those who don't want to even consider negotiations.

JOE KENNEDY: That I can't understand. It seems to me that the whole point of the diplomatic corps is to negotiate.

LADY ASTOR: Some are so angry with Hitler they don't want to find a diplomatic solution.

JOE KENNEDY: It's a terrible problem. I understand that many of the Jews have already left Germany and many more would like to leave.

LADY ASTOR: Now that the Nazis have annexed Austria, even more Jews will be trying to emigrate.

JOE KENNEDY: We must find a way to help them out of there.

LADY ASTOR: Lord Halifax opposes trying to get them out. He believes that we do a disservice by even offering the possibility of Jewish emigration out of Germany because it places pressure on the remaining Jews to leave.

JOE KENNEDY: No one would want to make things worse for those who stay.

LADY ASTOR: It is a complicated issue, Mr. Kennedy, and there is more to the story than is generally known.

JOE KENNEDY: How so?

LADY ASTOR: Just things that are not discussed. Things happened in the last war that are not discussed, and they won't be discussed.

JOE KENNEDY: That sounds like intrigue.

LADY ASTOR: We only hear part of the story. I just hope that war can be averted. That is my only hope. I've seen what happens when men go to war.

JOE KENNEDY: Lady Astor, I'll look forward to hearing more about your views.

LADY ASTOR: Then you must come out to Cliveden for a weekend. You and Mrs. Kennedy should bring your children out for some tennis and swimming. Do you like to ride a horse?

JOE KENNEDY: I ride every morning.

LADY ASTOR: You must come out. Have you met Charles Lindberg? You must meet him and hear what he has to say about the German Luftwaffe and then you must sit down with President Roosevelt and figure out a way to avoid another war.

Scene 7

Joseph Kennedy enters the Foreign Office in May 1938 with HAROLD ICKES, the Secretary of the Interior, to meet with Lord Halifax.

JOE KENNEDY: Mr. Ickes currently serves as the Secretary of the Interior.

HALIFAX: Do you administer the great territory of Alaska?

ICKES: Yes. It is a vast land with great economic potential.

HALIFAX: Has President Roosevelt proposed a Jewish colony in Alaska?

JOE KENNEDY: No, he has not and Mr. Ickes is not proposing anything today. I wanted to introduce him to you because a colony in Alaska seems like a reasonable solution under the circumstances. The government of the United States could facilitate a settlement there. I think we all realize that something must be done.

HALIFAX: The Jews do not pretend to be united on a solution. We know there is a very big problem in Germany, but I'm concerned that if we facilitate Nazi attempts to push German Jews to emigrate, the effect will be to push out Jews who don't wish to leave.

ICKES: I've been told that Great Britain promised the Jews a Jewish state in Palestine.

HALIFAX: You have been misinformed.

ICKES: Is the British government backing away from its commitment to establish a Jewish state?

HALIFAX: HIs Majesty's Government never made a commitment to establish a Jewish state.

ICKES: What was the Balfour Declaration?

HALIFAX: The Balfour Declaration was a letter signed by Secretary Balfour and approved by the Cabinet which stated that we would support the establishment of a national home for the Jewish people in Palestine. However, the letter clearly goes on to say that nothing would be done which would prejudice the civil and religious rights of the existing non-Jewish communities in Palestine. The problem is that Palestine has an existing population and the leadership there believes that the Jewish immigrants have violated the rights and taken the land of the existing residents of Palestine. The leaders of the Arab countries believe that the Palestinians are being treated as second class citizens in their own country.

JOE KENNEDY: Will the British government increase the quotas for Jewish immigration in Palestine?

HALIFAX: No government can give away someone else's country. We wanted the Jews to have a place where they could peacefully coexist with the existing population, but if it can't be done peacefully, we have no interest in forcing it on the Palestinians.

ICKES: I've been told that it was a contract between the government and the Zionists.

HALIFAX: There was never a contract.

JOE KENNEDY: I've never heard about a contract.

ICKES: I've heard that the Zionists helped the British and the British agreed to help the Zionists in return.

HALIFAX: Sir, let me assure you that this government does not have a contract with any Zionists and I am not aware of any written contract between any previous government and the Zionists.

ICKES: Have you heard of a lawyer named Samuel Landman-- an English Zionist?

HALIFAX: I am aware of Mr. Landman and of his positions. We have no contract with him.

JOE KENNEDY: Does he live in London?

HALIFAX: I think we all agree that time is of the essence. The Germans are angry with the Jewish people and the Nazis have made it very clear that they would like the German Jews, and now the Austrian Jews, to emigrate.

ICKES: The British restrict immigration to Palestine.

HALIFAX: Yes, and a large number will not be welcome in England, either. Is the United States prepared to accept possibly a million Jewish immigrants?

ICKES: We are recovering from a serious economic depression. A large Jewish immigration into the United States might prompt anti-Semitism, and there is some hostility toward Jews in the United States right now.

JOE KENNEDY: There is also hostility toward Catholics, but we are a country of immigrants. Maybe the answer is to offer many different possibilities. Maybe some Jews could go to Palestine, some to America, some to South America. Where in the British Empire might they go?

HALIFAX: We have had many discussions through the years with the Zionist leaders. There was talk of Kenya, but the Zionists are stuck on only permitting immigration to Palestine and that is not a reasonable possibility.

JOE KENNEDY: We need to come up with some destinations and we need to get the cooperation of the Nazi government. The Nazis now work to send the Jews to Madagascar.

ICKES: President Roosevelt is under great pressure to open Palestine.

HALIFAX: President Roosevelt does not administer Palestine. We must consider not only resolving Hitler's harassment of the Jewish people and where they might go but also of the security of the British Empire and our island home.

ICKES: You cannot be faulted for protecting the interests of your country, Lord Halifax, and our government must be committed to the security of the people of the United States.

JOE KENNEDY: If we can solve this problem of migration, we should be able to avoid a war. This must be our highest priority.

Scene 8

Joseph Kennedy is received by Ambassador JOACHIM VON RIBBENTROP at the German Embassy in London.

JOE KENNEDY: Congratulations on your new position.

VON RIBBENTROP: Thank you, sir.

JOE KENNEDY: As foreign minister, you will be working directly with Chancellor Hitler.

VON RIBBENTROP: I will.

JOE KENNEDY: You need to know that the government of the United States does not wish to enter any war involving the German Reich.

VON RIBBENTROP: Hopefully, there will be no war.

JOE KENNEDY: Hopefully not, but you should also understand the influence of the Jewish community in American politics. President Roosevelt has many Jewish friends in government and many more who have supported him for many years.

VON RIBBENTROP: We are very aware of the influence of the Jews in the democracies. We are most concerned about the negative press that we get in your newspapers. Aren't many of your newspapers owned by Jews?

JOE KENNEDY: That is probably so, but there is an effort at objective reporting.

VON RIBBENTROP: It's not hard to buy influence in a so-called democracy. Wasn't President Wilson compromised by a mistress?

JOE KENNEDY: That's ridiculous. Where do you hear such things? Wilson was a Sunday School teacher.

VON RIBBENTROP: He was a Sunday School teacher who was compromised by an extra-marital friendship and he didn't want to be exposed. He wrote love letters. Rumors were circulated that it was Brandeis who kept it quiet.

JOE KENNEDY: How can you possibly believe such a story!

VON RIBBENTROP: We don't want to believe it. The idea that a judge could make foreign policy is completely beyond our understanding of your government, and yet it happened.

JOE KENNEDY: I've never read anything about it.

VON RIBBENTROP: Exactly. The American press filters what is told to the American public. Do Americans understand that we are only trying to restore our country?

JOE KENNEDY: Well, you have stripped the Jews of citizenship in the Reich. Americans know that, but we don't understand why. Why do the Germans hate the Jews?

VON RIBBENTROP: The Germans don't hate the Jews. Jews have done very well in Germany for many generations. The records show that before we came to power, most justices in our courts in Berlin were Jewish; most doctors in our hospitals in Berlin were Jewish; most of the good business contracts went to Jewish businessmen. Jews are only one percent of our population and they have done very well in Germany.

JOE KENNEDY: So why would Herr Hitler take away their citizenship?

VON RIBBENTROP: The party does not consider the Jews to be loyal.

JOE KENNEDY: Jews served in the German army during the war.

VON RIBBENTROP: Some have been very loyal. Do you remember how the Germans were defeated in the Great War, sir?

JOE KENNEDY: I know what I heard about it in the United States. I managed a shipyard for the Navy during the war.

VON RIBBENTROP: Let me ask you a simple question: why did the United States enter the war?

JOE KENNEDY: Well, President Wilson rallied support for the idea of self-determination. He convinced Americans that we would be fighting the war to prevent all future wars. It was going to be the end of colonialism.

VON RIBBENTROP: Yes, and do you remember that the Germans sued for peace before the American entry into the war?

JOE KENNEDY: I remember that there were discussions about whether the war should be ended. Yes.

VON RIBBENTROP: Then the newspapers in America swung support for American entry into the war. Have you heard of Mr. Samuel Landman?

JOE KENNEDY: His name keeps coming up as I learn more about this conflict.

VON RIBBENTROP: Mr. Landman was a Zionist lawyer during the Great War.

JOE KENNEDY: I didn't know that.

VON RIBBENTROP: Mr. Landman has been so kind as to write down exactly why the Americans entered the war against Germany. I suggest you read his arguments. He points out that the Zionists conspired with the British to prompt American entry into the war on the British side. The Zionists would rally support for the British cause and the British would help the Zionists create a homeland for the Jews in Palestine.

JOE KENNEDY: I have never heard such a claim.

VON RIBBENTROP: No?

JOE KENNEDY: What makes you believe that such a conspiracy is true?

VON RIBBENTROP: Surely you have heard of the Balfour Declaration, Ambassador Kennedy.

JOE KENNEDY: I have, of course.

VON RIBBENTROP: According to Mr. Landman, the Zionist lawyer, the Balfour Declaration was the public acknowledgement of Britain's commitment to help establish a Jewish homeland in Palestine. The Balfour Declaration was issued because the British were satisfied that the Zionists had performed on their end of the contract.

JOE KENNEDY: What contract?

VON RIBBENTROP: The contract was a *quid pro quo* agreement that the Zionists would prompt American entry into the war in exchange for the British helping them enter Palestine. So argues the Zionist lawyer, Mr. Landman.

JOE KENNEDY: Americans have never heard of such a contract.

VON RIBBENTROP: Mr. Ambassador, you would have had to have lived in Germany during those years to understand the misery of the German people during that war. We were completely unaware of the deal between the Zionists and the British at that time. After the British promised the Jews Palestine, German Jews worked to defeat Germany from within our country. Their newspapers found fault with our generals; their labor leaders organized strikes at our munitions plants; and at the end, when we were weakest, they staged a revolution. Returning German troops had to fight for control of their own country from the Judeo-Bolsheviks. After we surrendered, our people were denied food. Many starved. German woman and children starved during the embargo while Germany's Jews were fed by so called international relief organizations. Many German people died because the Allies insisted on a treaty which had nothing to do with President Wilson's promise of self-determination. The treaty stripped Germany of her land and much of her population. We were double crossed.

JOE KENNEDY: Do you you believe Germany's Jews were involved?

VON RIBBENTROP: The Zionists were clearly involved. A million American soldiers were brought to the front to defeat Germany. More were on the way.

JOE KENNEDY: If we believe Mr. Landman's statement.

VON RIBBENTROP: The Zionists made a deal with the British to get their own homeland. Hitler embraces their idea. Hitler wants them to leave Germany and go to Palestine, and Germany can resume being the homeland of the Germans.

JOE KENNEDY: I don't agree with you on that, Ambassador von Ribbentrop. You must remember that very few Jews want to go to Palestine. If you have a successful business in the United States or England or Germany, you don't necessarily want to give that up to go to Palestine.

VON RIBBENTROP: That was why they betrayed the German nation. The Jews wanted a homeland.

JOE KENNEDY: Surely you can't think that all of Germany's Jews agreed on some secret plan. I'll bet almost none have them have even heard of that plan—even now.

VON RIBBENTROP: Some of them clearly did.

JOE KENNEDY: Americans don't want a war and I don't think the British do either. Prime Minister Chamberlain understands your concerns and I believe he wants to help you.

VON RIBBENTROP: You should remember this: Chancellor Hitler can be a wonderful fellow. He can be generous and reasonable but he has come to power by imposing deadlines and insisting on outcomes. He can be reasonable up to a point, then he becomes decisive and very stubborn.

JOE KENNEDY: I'm going to meet with President Roosevelt next week. I'm glad I had a chance to hear your views, sir. I think I understand this issue better now.

Scene 9

Joseph Kennedy meets with President Roosevelt at Hyde Park in June 1938.

JOE KENNEDY: It is extremely serious. If we don't make a deal with Hitler, we're going to regret it.

ROOSEVELT: My advisers say that we shouldn't have negotiations with dictators. That's our official policy.

JOE KENNEDY: Who should diplomats talk to if they don't talk to our enemies? I spend enough time enjoying nice dinners with the aristocrats. Somebody needs to cut through the nonsense and get to the bottom of this. What's the point of diplomacy?

ROOSEVELT: Some Jews are already leaving Germany and ending up in Palestine.

JOE KENNEDY: That's what I've learned. Jews with one thousand pounds can get into Palestine without violating the British quota. The Jews buy a thousand pounds' worth of German products and the products and the owners then are reunited in Palestine. There, the Jews sell their German made products and get the cash. This arrangement boils down to the Jews being able to get their property out of Germany.

ROOSEVELT: Hitler is holding them hostage and he's getting around the boycott.

JOE KENNEDY: Exactly. The British allow the Jews into Palestine if they bring a thousand pounds and the Nazis let them leave. I assume that everyone takes a cut along the way.

ROOSEVELT: The numbers have not been large.

JOE KENNEDY: That's right. We're only talking about tens of thousands, but the number of Jews who want to leave is probably much higher now. The Austrian Jews need to get out as well.

ROOSEVELT: Do you believe that our boycott of the Germans is potentially dangerous?

JOE KENNEDY: Mr. President, I see a terrifying problem. Hitler is angry at the Jews. I've heard a lot of reasons why he might be; let's just say that he is. He is in complete control of what goes in and out of Germany and Austria. Nothing is going to happen unless he says so. Chamberlain recognizes that he's going to have to reverse some of the punitive measures taken against Germany after the last war. Hitler feels like he must move quickly before the French and the English have a chance to modernize their weapons. So, I see the situation as being quite unstable and I see the Jews in a very vulnerable position. If we could figure out a way for the Jews to leave Germany and Austria, then I think we could defuse the entire problem.

ROOSEVELT: How?

JOE KENNEDY: I think we should expand the agreement that the Nazis have in place. To do that, we must get some money together to pay expenses and we must have a place to ship them. Lord Halifax tells me that something could be worked out in Kenya.

ROOSEVELT: The British don't want a large influx of Jews into England---

JOE KENNEDY: --and the State Department doesn't want a large influx into America, but they need to go somewhere and probably fast. So I say we just get them out of harm's way: Kenya, Alaska, California, South America, wherever we can get them safely and start today.

ROOSEVELT: Why not Palestine?

JOE KENNEDY: There is an existing population in Palestine and the people there claim that the Jews are already violating their rights.

ROOSEVELT: Our Jewish friends here think that if we apply pressure, the British will clear out Palestine for incoming Jews.

JOE KENNEDY: How would that work? The British load the Arab population onto trains at gunpoint and transport them away from their homes and villages? Take them out of their country? Where would they go?

ROOSEVELT: Doesn't sound like a good way to make friends with the Arabs.

JOE KENNEDY: The Arabs ship the British most of their oil. We must find some places for the Jews to relocate-- the Jews who want to relocate.

ROOSEVELT: There is no sentiment in this country to mobilize for a war-- quite the opposite. Most Americans think we got tricked into getting into the last one.

JOE KENNEDY: The Nazis agree with them.

ROOSEVELT: We need to convene an international conference to address the issue of emigration.

JOE KENNEDY: We need to start negotiating with Hitler. We need a new understanding.

ROOSEVELT: The American Jewish community doesn't support negotiations.

JOE KENNEDY: We need to talk to them. Whatever we're doing is not enough.

ROOSEVELT: I hear that you are interested in running for president.

JOE KENNEDY: (laughs) I'm not interested in running if you will seek re-election. I told the reporters just the other day that I wouldn't even admit interest while I am serving in this Administration. I will wait to hear about your plans. I do have some opinions about how to resolve the biggest issues of the day: we must avoid another European war.

ROOSEVELT: I'll look forward to seeing you at the White House for dinner tomorrow night. I appreciate you reporting what you have learned. Remember that I have a lot of people to satisfy here and no two of them think the same way about Europe.

Scene 10

Joseph Kennedy, Jr. and his younger brother John F. Kennedy chase after some attractive young women on the French Riviera in the summer of 1938. Ambassador Kennedy holds up his hand and his sons stop the pursuit.

JOE KENNEDY: Could you boys show a little restraint? The Secretary of the Treasury is visiting today.

JOE JUNIOR: We met his children.

JOE KENNEDY: I want both of you to be around for the cocktail hour but watch what you say.

JOE JUNIOR: Sir?

JOE KENNEDY: Just be careful about quoting me. You should remember that Secretary Morgenthau reports everything he hears to the President. Joe, I want you to go down and make sure your brother Bobby is not terrorizing everyone in the swimming pool. Those Morgenthau children might not be accustomed to the abuse they will experience here. Jack, I want you to walk with me for a few minutes.

JOE JUNIOR: All right. (He leaves.)

JOE KENNEDY: (to JFK) Are you getting enough to eat, son?

JACK: You know I'm working on it.

JOE KENNEDY: Your mother says you won't drink the milk.

JACK: It stinks. Smells spoiled to me.

JOE KENNEDY: Drink it anyway. It just hasn't been pasteurized. You need that milk fat. Did you have a chance to look up the lawyer Samuel Landman?

JACK: Yes. Landman wrote a little booklet called "Great Britain, the Jews, and Palestine" a couple of years ago. Published in London.

JOE KENNEDY: Give me the summary.

JACK: Well, Landman claims to have been the lawyer for the Zionist Organization at the time of the Balfour Declaration; so you'd have to say the man knows what he is talking about. The pamphlet is an appeal to the British government to avoid having a parliament for Palestine. The British tried to set up a legislative body but Landman argues that this would give the Arab population the means to cut off further Jewish immigration. That's the reason he wrote it, but his argument amazed me.

JOE KENNEDY: How so?

JACK: Landman says that the Balfour Declaration was the second half of a deal between the Zionists and the British government. He believes that the Balfour Declaration guaranteed the Jews a home in Palestine.

JOE KENNEDY: What was the first part of the deal?

JACK: That's what amazed me. He says that there was a *quid pro quo* contract between the Zionists and the British that if the Zionists used their influence to get the United States into the war, the British would help them secure a non-exclusive homeland in Palestine. Landman says that the American Zionist influence, whatever that means, convinced President Wilson to enter the war.

JOE KENNEDY: I still don't believe it.

JACK: It doesn't say how the Zionists got the United States to enter the war, just says that they did and the British now need to follow through with their commitment to Jewish immigration to Palestine. He says it was a "gentlemen's agreement."

JOE KENNEDY: Right. If Americans were to find out about that pamphlet, we might see some very serious anti-Semitism right in our own country. Nobody I knew who went to the Great War thought they were doing it to create a Jewish homeland.

JACK: Landman asserts that the reason the Nazis are so angry with the Jews is because the Zionists got America into the war to beat Germany.

JOE KENNEDY: Landman says that?

JACK: Right. He says that the Jews are in a tight spot in Germany since the Nazis know about the deal and the British haven't secured Palestine for the Jews.

JOE KENNEDY: That makes sense.

JACK: I can't believe we haven't read about this in the press back home.

JOE KENNEDY: Well, I can believe it. There's more management of the news than we think. That deal wouldn't play very well back home. Don't bring it up again unless I ask you to.

JACK: Yes, sir.

JOE KENNEDY: Don't even mention it to your brother Joe or your mother.

JACK: Yes, sir.

Scene 11

Joseph Kennedy stands with Secretary of the Treasury Henry Morgenthau, Jr. as they watch their children in Southern France.

JOE KENNEDY: England has a quota on the number of immigrants they will take, as does America, but given the pressing circumstances, I've tried to initiate some discussions about where the refugees, primarily Jews, will settle.

MORGENTHAU: A very important question. I'm concerned that Cordell Hull and his State Department are afflicted with the virus "anti-Semiticus."

JOE KENNEDY: That raises the question of what constitutes an anti-Semite?

MORGENTHAU: Not a well-defined term.

JOE KENNEDY: I think we can agree that Herr Hitler is an anti-Semite, but what about people who don't support Zionism. Are they anti-Semites?

MORGENTHAU: Well, given the fact that my own father, Henry Morgenthau, Senior, does not support Zionism, I'm inclined to say no. Most American Jews are not Zionists.

JOE KENNEDY: What about Lord Halifax? He is an honorable man, an aristocrat who has the confidence of the King, but he doesn't believe that England has an obligation to accept the Jews from Germany. Is he an anti-Semite?

MORGENTHAU: I'd have to say that an anti-Semite is someone who wishes bad things for the Jews—because they are Jews. Someone who simply doesn't favor a large immigration to England doesn't make him an anti-Semite. Keep in mind that no one in the United States is arguing for increased Jewish immigration. We can't all be anti-Semites.

JOE KENNEDY: What about historical documents? If a historical document could cause trouble for the Jews, would release of the document be an act of anti-Semitism?

MORGENTHAU: No. I'd argue that a historical document would have to be judged on its own merits. It might not be a real

51

document.   Its contents might be disputed—that's happened before-- but I would have to say that a historical document, an authentic document which is not intended to cause the Jews harm, would not be by itself anti-Semitic.   Do you have something in mind, Joe?

JOE KENNEDY: I stumble on things here and there-- I'm sure we all do. There's a lot of history here in Europe and there is anger.

MORGENTHAU: I'd say that if you are part of the process of trying to get the Jews to safety, as you are, you are never going to be judged an anti-Semite. Do you think we can get rid of Hitler?

JOE KENNEDY: I don't see how. I'm told that he has built up a modern army and air force. We don't even have that in the United States. The British have still not rearmed.

MORGENTHAU: I'm worried.

JOE KENNEDY: I'm told that Hitler has promised to reunite the German people. He believes that Germany was unfairly victimized by the peace treaty and he is determined to bring the German people back under German rule.

MORGENTHAU: If they can be trusted.

JOE KENNEDY: Right, but that's not a determination they are asking us to make. Hitler is intent on restoring the German nation.

MORGENTHAU: What's the answer?

JOE KENNEDY: I don't have the answer yet, but I can tell you one thing for sure: no one is going to leave Germany or Austria without Hitler's permission. So, if we want to get people out of there, Jews or Catholics, we need to make some deals and keep the peace. Wars have a way of closing borders as I'm sure you know.

MORGENTHAU: Can we stand by and watch the Germans persecute the German Jews?

JOE KENNEDY: What choice do we have? Are we going to attack Germany? The Neutrality Acts don't allow us to even take sides in European conflicts.

MORGENTHAU: Hitler acts like a criminal.

JOE KENNEDY: We all agree he is an evil man in a powerful position, but we face some very real problems and we need to work with him to get the Jews out of there.

MORGENTHAU: We can't make friends with someone who denies people civil rights because of their religion.

JOE KENNEDY: If you were a Jew stuck in Germany wouldn't you want us to get you out?

MORGENTHAU: Of course.

JOE KENNEDY: Then tell me how we can do that without talking with Hitler.

MORGENTHAU: We've got to get rid of him.

JOE KENNEDY: That isn't going to happen. Tell me how we are going to get those German or Austrian Jews out without negotiating with Hitler.

MORGENTHAU: We can't negotiate with criminals.

JOE KENNEDY: Diplomacy is more like business than you fellows seem to think. In business, you don't need to like someone to make an agreement. You need to be pleasant. You need to be polite. You might want to flatter someone you are doing business with, but in the end, you want to get the business transacted. You want to have an exchange.

MORGENTHAU: What are you proposing, Joe?

JOE KENNEDY: I think we must negotiate with the Nazis.

Scene 12

Joseph Kennedy, dressed in formal attire, stands near an open box on a table and lifts out a gas mask in September 1938. A telephone is on the table while across the room a male secretary waits on a telephone. Rosemary Kennedy enters the room as her attendant and her mother follow her.

ROSEMARY: I'm not going to put on a mask.

ROSE: Now, dear. Listen to your father.

JOE KENNEDY: Rosemary, you and I are going to stay here in London and your mother and the others are going back to New York.

ROSEMARY: Why do we have to stay?

JOE KENNEDY: Well, I work in London and the President doesn't want me to come home yet. You have made very nice friends in your school here and the nuns hate to see your progress interrupted. I need someone to come with me if I am asked to dinner with the King and Queen.

ROSEMARY: Would I get to see the King and Queen again?

JOE KENNEDY: Maybe.   We must see what happens here in London. (Rosemary walks out with her attendant.)

Secretary: (into telephone)   I'm waiting to speak to your district supervisor.

ROSE: When do you know if we should leave?

JOE KENNEDY: I think we should assume that things are not safe here for you and the children.

ROSE: I thought there was still hope.

JOE KENNEDY: The Prime Minister is not hopeful. Gas masks are being distributed all over the city.

Secretary: Yes, please stand by for United States Ambassador Joseph Kennedy.

JOE KENNEDY: (into telephone) Yes. We planned for a train to take American citizens to meet a Swedish ship at Leith. I've just been informed by the company that the Firth of Forth has been mined. They can't get to Leith. (He pauses.) Right, but they are willing to pick up the passengers from Newcastle. Can the train be re-routed to Newcastle? ... Yes. Excellent. I will remind the Prime Minister of your helpfulness. I appreciate it.

JOE KENNEDY: (to secretary) Make sure all those Americans get on the right train. I'm holding you responsible. (Secretary leaves.)

ROSE: (trying on a gas mask) I hate to think of you being here by yourself if they are dropping poison gas.

JOE KENNEDY: That makes two of us, but it shouldn't go quite that fast. Unless the British drop gas on Berlin, I don't think the Germans will drop gas on London.

ROSE: What are they doing in Washington?

JOE KENNEDY: The President has apparently sent a second telegram to Hitler arguing that once the discussions stop and the fighting begins, it will be a terrible blow against humanity. He's sent two telegrams but we should have solved this problem already. When there was time, they didn't want me talking to Hitler-- because Germany is mistreating its Jews. How does that help us now? How did that help the Jews? Everybody would have been better off if we'd made a deal.

Scene 13

Neville Chamberlain descends the steps of a plane which has returned him from Munich. He reads from a piece of paper.

"We, the German Führer and Chancellor, and the British Prime Minister, have had a further meeting today and are agreed in recognizing that the question of Anglo-German relations is of the first importance for our two countries and for Europe. We regard the agreement signed last night and the Anglo-German Naval Agreement as symbolic of the desire of our two peoples never to go to war with one another again. We are resolved that the method of consultation shall be the method adopted to deal with any other questions that may concern our two countries, and we are determined to continue our efforts to remove possible sources of difference, and thus to contribute to assure the peace of Europe."

"I believe it is peace for our time..."

Act II

Scene 1

Joseph Kennedy enters the office of Prime Minister Neville Chamberlain following the Prime Minister's return from Munich in early October 1938. Lord Halifax greets Kennedy with the Prime Minister.

JOE KENNEDY: What a great victory for you in Munich!

CHAMBERLAIN: (looks at Lord Halifax) We are relieved that Herr Hitler signed the agreement.

HALIFAX: War has been averted.

JOE KENNEDY: President Roosevelt cabled his congratulations.

CHAMBERLAIN: Hitler has incorporated Austria into his Reich and now has united the German nationals living in Czechoslovakia with Germany. His only remaining objective will be to regain Danzig.

HALIFAX: In time, he should get those areas without the dramatic display we have seen with Czechoslovakia.

JOE KENNEDY: To be able remove the sources of conflict using politics rather than violence relieves all of Europe from a horrible war.

CHAMBERLAIN: Still, we have our critics right here in England.

HALIFAX: Duff Cooper has resigned from the Admiralty. Churchill rattles his sword. He won't rest until millions of young men have returned to the trenches in France.

CHAMBERLAIN: Who prompts Churchill to such agitation? The situation has been defused and if we can just manage to get the Germans in Danzig back under Hitler's rule, we will have a much more stable peace.

JOE KENNEDY: Let me say once again what a great moment this is. During times of peace we can negotiate our differences.

CHAMBERLAIN: Thank you.

JOE KENNEDY: The President continues to be under great pressure to help open up Palestine.

Chamberlain and Halifax look at each other for a long moment.

CHAMBERLAIN: I'm sure he is but His Majesty's Government never agreed to displace Arabs in the service of any other people. Any commitment we have ever made, any encouragement, has been with the understanding that the rights of existing populations would be strictly observed.

JOE KENNEDY: That's right.

HALIFAX: The rights of the existing Arab populations have not been strictly observed and the Arab leaders are justifiably concerned.

CHAMBERLAIN: This government will not forcefully remove an Arab population from a land they have occupied for eighteen centuries.

HALIFAX: There is also a question of our strategic security: without oil, we cannot defend England.

CHAMBERLAIN: So even if we believed that moving an Arab population out of Palestine was an ethical thing to do--

HALIFAX: --which we do not believe---

CHAMBERLAIN: --to do so would imperil our supply of oil and our security as a nation.

JOE KENNEDY: Probably so.

CHAMBERLAIN: A different solution must be conceived and the leadership for accepting that solution should probably come from the United States.

HALIFAX: President Roosevelt could do the world a great service to propose a reasonable solution to this question.

JOE KENNEDY: It will be a great challenge.

CHAMBERLAIN: As you have said, solving the refugee problem is critical to preserving the peace.

HALIFAX: The Prime Minister and I realize your great potential to help us with this question. You should come up with something workable, have it debated in the United States, and approved by President Roosevelt.

CHAMBERLAIN: Realize that our options in Palestine are limited.

HALIFAX: Existing populations will not voluntarily abandon their homes in the service of refugees from Europe.

CHAMBERLAIN: Not peacefully. Land might be purchased over time-- but not immediately. New solutions must be proposed.

Scene 2

President Roosevelt meets with Henry Morgenthau in the White House on October 20, 1938.

ROOSEVELT: I have no idea who authorized the speech, but Cordell should be here any minute.

MORGENTHAU: Why would Kennedy even be asked to speak at Trafalgar Day?

ROOSEVELT: Apparently, he was the first American ambassador ever to be asked. It was an occasion to discuss how our navy will always have a special kinship with the Royal Navy-- that sort of thing.

(Carrying a copy of the New York Times, Secretary of State CORDELL HULL enters with SUMNER WELLS and J. P. MOFFAT, assistant secretaries.)

HULL: Have you seen this?

ROOSEVELT: I've heard it's not good.

HULL: Let me just read from the coverage in the New York Times. Kennedy said that he "did not want to talk about a little theory of mine..."

MORGENTHAU: I like that: he disavows what he is about to say.

HULL: (reading from the paper)   "...a little theory of mine that it is unproductive for both democratic and dictator countries to widen the division now existing between them by emphasizing their differences, which are self-apparent."

ROOSEVELT: Well, that isn't so bad, my friends.

HULL: No, he goes on. "Instead of hammering away at what are regarded as irreconcilables, they can advantageously bend their energies toward solving their remaining common problems and attempt to re-establish good relations on a world basis...After all, we have to live together in the same world, whether we like it or not."

ROOSEVELT: That's it? Read me the bad part.

HULL: That's what he said but look at this headline in the Times: "Kennedy for amity with fascist bloc: Urges that democracies and dictatorships forget their differences in outlook.   Calls for disarmament."

MORGENTHAU: Mr. President, don't you see that Kennedy is trying to change our foreign policy?

ROOSEVELT: I don't think we'll invite Mr. Hitler over for dinner, but Joe seems to be saying we should try to find some common ground, maybe soften relations with the Germans. Did Joe use the word 'disarmament?'

MORGENTHAU: It's outrageous! The Nazis are criminals.

HULL: They break the most fundamental laws.

ROOSEVELT: Joe isn't saying that he likes the Germans and he isn't trying to excuse their behavior

MORGENTHAU: He's trying to make friends.

ROOSEVELT: I suppose so.

MORGENTHAU: The Times says his statement is an excellent summary of the policies of Prime Minister Neville Chamberlain.

ROOSEVELT: That is probably true. I think the British government is trying to reduce tensions.

MORGENTHAU: We cannot negotiate with dictators.

HULL: Our policy has been to quarantine them, Mr. President.

ROOSEVELT: We're not changing that. We're not going to approve what is going on in Germany.

MORGENTHAU: We shouldn't.

HULL: And we won't.

ROOSEVELT: Who approved that speech?

HULL: (turning to Wells) Who approved that speech?

WELLS: (turning to Moffat) I've been working on Mexico. I thought you'd been looking at Kennedy's speeches.

HULL: (turning to Moffat) Haven't you been keeping an eye on Kennedy?

MOFFAT: I screen what he sends me. I think these comments were made off the cuff. Don't you think the Times has taken them rather far? Joe is just saying that we ought to look for ways to be able to negotiate again.

HULL: That's outrageous. We're not going to become friends with the Nazis.

MOFFAT: I will assume responsibility if responsibility is to be assigned.

HULL: Somebody is going to have to reign in Joe Kennedy.

MORGENTHAU: Has our foreign policy changed? Should we make friends with a government which is persecuting religious minorities?

ROOSEVELT: Our policy hasn't changed.

HULL: Mr. President, I'll have a statement prepared for you to deliver on this subject. Maybe we can repair some of this damage.

ROOSEVELT: Doesn't Arthur Krock still work at the New York Times?

MORGENTHAU: Yes. I believe he does.

ROOSEVELT: Isn't he the fellow who is managing Kennedy's press relations?

MORGENTHAU: Informally. I think Joe pays him quite well.

ROOSEVELT: Well, he hasn't helped Joe here. The Times is killing him with that headline.

HULL: We will just have you say that there can be "no peace with nations that threaten war as an instrument of national policy and persecute and deny freedom of speech and religion to their own citizens."

MORGENTHAU: That should do.

ROOSEVELT: I think he was just trying to be helpful.

HULL: The problem is that tensions are so high that every phrase gets scrutinized.

MORGENTHAU: You can't have ambassadors making policy. Policy must be made at this level and ambassadors must carry out policies.

ROOSEVELT: I think the Times is pressing rather hard on this. He wasn't saying that we should "forget our differences." They made that phrase up.

HULL: We'll still have to clarify the situation.

ROOSEVELT: No. I understand that, but I think we should quietly get word to the Times that we don't expect to be attacked every time someone calls for a peaceful approach.

MORGENTHAU: He can't change policy.

ROOSEVELT: You should remember Henry that I don't have a lock on this office. The American public doesn't want to fight another war in Europe.

MORGENTHAU: I'm not calling for a war.

ROOSEVELT: No, I understand that, but if we are pressed not to negotiate with our enemies, there is little chance of anything but a war. Kennedy is just trying to re-engage with the Germans.

MORGENTHAU: There are people who think he should be recalled from his post.

ROOSEVELT: That's right and there are people who think that he is doing a great job there by trying to prevent a war from breaking out. Now, I don't want him back here running for president, possibly with the criticism that I'm under too much special influence.

MORGENTHAU: Yes, Mr. President. I agree with you.

HULL: I'll have that statement prepared, Mr. President. We'll make sure that they understand that there can be no peace with nations that threaten their own citizens on religious grounds.

ROOSEVELT: Make sure it's something we can live with, something we can run on. I'll talk to Joe.

Scene 3

World Zionist Organization President CHAIM WEIZMANN meets with Joseph Kennedy at the American Embassy in London in late October 1938.

JOE KENNEDY: I must tell you some news you are not going to want to hear.

WEIZMANN: What news is that?

JOE KENNEDY: From what I've heard, the British will restrict further Jewish immigration into Palestine.

WEIZMANN: That's what we understand.

JOE KENNEDY: The Prime Minister and Lord Halifax told me that the British government will not forcefully remove Arabs from Palestine.

WEIZMANN: No one is asking them to do that.

JOE KENNEDY: Well, I'm sure you know Jabotinsky. He's from Russia as I know you are.

WEIZMANN: He has founded a different movement within Zionism.

JOE KENNEDY: Jabotinsky tells me that the Arabs aren't going to simply leave Palestine. The Jews will need to force them off their property.

WEIZMANN: We do not share the same vision for the future.

JOE KENNEDY: He advocates force.

WEIZMANN: I do not. I like the idea of paying for property.

JOE KENNEDY: The Arabs are not going to get up and leave their property in Palestine. It isn't going to happen and the British are not going to force them to leave.

WEIZMANN: Do you see the Arabs being willing to accept inducements?

JOE KENNEDY: Yes, I do, but that process will take time. What I see is that Hitler wants the Jews to leave Germany. On that can we agree?

WEIZMANN: No doubt about that.

JOE KENNEDY: There is a program in Germany to allow certain Jews to leave-- to be transferred to Palestine with some of their property.

WEIZMANN: That is a very sensitive program but you're right.

JOE KENNEDY: A Transfer Agreement.

WEIZMANN: That's right.

JOE KENNEDY: Now, trouble brews in Palestine. The Arabs are resisting, objecting to being moved off from their land.

WEIZMANN: We buy the land.

JOE KENNEDY: Nothing goes off perfectly in a situation like this. How can it? The big point is that the Jews feel that they are attacked. The Arabs feel that they are attacked. There is violence. Killings. That has already happened.

WEIZMANN: There are problems.

JOE KENNEDY: Problems are sparked with the immigration of tens of thousands of Jews. Imagine if that number were much greater. If we see violence when the number of immigrants has been in the tens of thousands, what might happen when hundreds of thousands want to enter?

WEIZMANN: The British promised to open up Palestine.

JOE KENNEDY: Whatever the British promised, we must now devise a workable solution. It isn't going to be Palestine in the next few years. We should create a transfer agreement for Jews to get to the United States and South America and Africa and anywhere else they are able to go.

WEIZMANN: They will encounter more anti-Semitism anywhere they go. If they go to South America, eventually anti-Semitism will increase. The answer to this historic anti-Semitism is for the Jews to go home, to Palestine, and build a country there.

JOE KENNEDY: That's the Zionist vision, I understand, but they can't go to Palestine if they don't have land to receive them. It will take time to buy that land. In the meantime, my Jewish friends in Florida aren't doing so badly. We get by.

WEIZMANN: We never said we were not going to pay for the land.

JOE KENNEDY: We're here to find a solution that will work in the next few years, a solution that will allow Jews in Germany to get out-- hopefully with some of their property. We need a deal with Hitler. If he doesn't want them there, he should allow them to leave.

WEIZMANN: With their property.

JOE KENNEDY: Yes, with their property if they can get out with their property.

WEIZMANN: They should go to Palestine.

JOE KENNEDY: Dr. Weizmann, if I were in Germany, I'd go anywhere else. Property or no property, Palestine or Alaska. I'd want the opportunity to get out.

WEIZMANN: You'd allow those Nazis to take your money, Mr. Kennedy?

JOE KENNEDY: I wouldn't like it—no-- but what we are facing is a man, a dictator, who thinks the Jews have taken more than their share in Germany. You and I do not agree with that, but he is not asking for a debate. Why not pay whatever exit tax they ask and get a place in California? That's what I'd want, and I'd want an American Ambassador in London trying to make that possible. If I wanted to go to Palestine, I'd give the developers some time to buy property and build houses there and then I'd go to Palestine. In the short term, believe me, it is tough to beat Florida.

WEIZMANN: You have proposed that we try to be friends with the Nazis. How can you be friends with a man like Hitler?

JOE KENNEDY: We're not being friends. I'm saying that we need to talk to him, to find common ground, to make an agreement. Do you realize that if we don't make a deal with Hitler the world could be pushed into another war?

WEIZMANN: You would meet with him?

JOE KENNEDY: Damn right, I would. How else are we going to reach that understanding? Somebody needs to get to him; somebody needs to find out what kind of deal he'll take. An agreement now allows Jews to migrate to Palestine. The Zionists made that deal with Hitler. Why not let me extend that arrangement to other countries?

WEIZMANN: Would that proposal need to be approved by Washington?

JOE KENNEDY: We can't wait for Washington.

WEIZMANN: He's a malicious dictator.

JOE KENNEDY: He is that. No laws are enforced in wartime. The Jews in Germany will have even fewer rights than they have today. In the last war, there was starvation. While the Allies pushed the Germans to accept the terms of the Treaty of Versailles, women and children starved to death. If we have another war, who do you think Hitler will allow to starve first?

WEIZMANN: He won't spare the Jews.

JOE KENNEDY: That's right. The best thing we can do for them is keep talking. Good things can happen during peacetime. People can sell their property and move to other countries. That isn't going to happen in a war.

Scene 4

Prime Minister Neville Chamberlain and Foreign Secretary Lord Halifax meet in the prime minister's office on November 12, 1938, just after news of the Kristallnacht reached London. They are looking over newspapers and reports.

CHAMBERLAIN: My God, my God. What has become of Germany?

HALIFAX: It is unspeakable.

CHAMBERLAIN: This tragedy in Germany could bring our government down.

HALIFAX: Why should we be held responsible?

CHAMBERLAIN: Jewish shops plundered. Men pulled out of their homes and assaulted. Synagogues destroyed.

HALIFAX: All of this grows out of the excesses of the last war. Had we made peace when the Germans sued for peace, there would have been no Russian Revolution, the Kaiser would not have fallen, and the impossible terms of the peace would not have been imposed. We would have never heard of Hitler.

CHAMBERLAIN: We can't change any of that now.

HALIFAX: No, indeed not, but the decision to bring the Americans into that war and the decision to starve the Germans into submission now have come home.

CHAMBERLAIN: We did not make those decisions.

HALIFAX: No and they were terrible mistakes.

CHAMBERLAIN: We must proceed knowing how we got here but making the best decisions we can under the circumstances.

HALIFAX: Why do you believe that we will be held accountable for how the Nazis have mistreated their Jews?

CHAMBERLAIN: I'm afraid it is all politics. We will be blamed for not going to war with Hitler rather than trying to solve his demands peacefully.

HALIFAX: Our crime is to attempt to avoid a war?

CHAMBERLAIN: Our critics are now complaining that I am not courageous—not up to the fight with the young Hitler.

HALIFAX: Warmongers always throw in the challenge of courage, don't they? How many Jews would suffer if we were even to impose harsh sanctions on the Nazis? It is not at all clear what we should do, even now.

CHAMBERLAIN: We should prepare for war.

HALIFAX: We should always be prepared for war.

CHAMBERLAIN: Yes, of course, but in a peacetime economy, it seems like such a waste to build the tanks and airplanes to wage war. It will take a year or more to just obtain the basic tools of a strong defense.

HALIFAX: We must do that.

CHAMBERLAIN: I'd rather put the investment into improving relations than into gathering weapons.

HALIFAX: It seems that Hitler is forcing us to produce the tools of war.

(The Secretary announces the arrival of Ambassador Kennedy.)

Secretary: His Excellency, Ambassador Kennedy.

CHAMBERLAIN: Terrible news, I'm afraid.

JOE KENNEDY: Tragic.

CHAMBERLAIN: This will push us in the direction of war.

JOE KENNEDY: I'm afraid it will, but war will only make matters worse.

HALIFAX: The backbench will revolt with this news. It will be taken as a sign that peaceful solutions have failed. Churchill presses for a return of the army to Europe.

CHAMBERLAIN: I wonder what well equipped army he is dreaming about. We lack the arms to defend the home island.

HALIFAX: We have ordered more planes and tanks.

JOE KENNEDY: Now, everyone wants more guns and planes, but it will take time.

CHAMBERLAIN: We will not able to use them in Czechoslovakia or anywhere else in Eastern Europe. It is one thing to have them in England and another to have them in Prague.

HALIFAX: If we could solve the question of the refugees, we could decompress the tensions.

JOE KENNEDY: President Roosevelt has heard suggestions for months which attempt to answer this problem. Former President Herbert Hoover and Roosevelt's old friend Bernard Baruch, a Republican and a Democrat, have been advancing a so called "United States of Africa."

HALIFAX: Anthony Gustav de Rothschild has worked on that project here in London. We know his proposal.

JOE KENNEDY: The Administration has negotiators and others working here on the refugee commissions to figure out ways to allow the Jews to go to Venezuela and Costa Rica. Mexico, Brazil, and Haiti have been mentioned; possibly Portuguese Angola.

CHAMBERLAIN: We are aware of these efforts, but no one has championed the cause.

JOE KENNEDY: The Zionists keep pushing for Palestine.

HALIFAX: That would be a great suggestion if Palestine was an empty land. It is not, and the existing population feels that the new immigrants are pushing them off from their property, killing Arabs, and claiming self-defense.

JOE KENNEDY: This purging of Jews in Germany, this new act of aggression demands a new response.

CHAMBERLAIN: Surely your president will want to be heard on this.

JOE KENNEDY: Everyone will want to be heard. But we must take the initiative. This is our opportunity.

HALIFAX: What exactly do you propose?

JOE KENNEDY: We must set up a program to pay Hitler to allow the Jews of Germany to emigrate. There is already a plan in place for them to go to Palestine, but it isn't happening fast enough. Other countries must be made available.

CHAMBERLAIN: What about Palestine?

JOE KENNEDY: Yes, but Palestine can't accept tens of thousands of Jews today, to say nothing of the three or four hundred thousand Jews in Germany who need to emigrate. So, we must set up a new program and get the process started. Each country needs to realize the extent of this humanitarian problem and accept Jews emigrating from Germany.

CHAMBERLAIN: You see that this government is not willing to do to the existing population in Palestine what the Germans are threatening to do in Poland.

HALIFAX: We will not push them off their property.

CHAMBERLAIN: The solution lies with getting the Jews to safety or at least to start an organized effort. How do you know that Hitler will cooperate? I have found him most stubborn.

JOE KENNEDY: Money. This program is going to cost some money, but if it is money that would allow us to avoid a war, it is money well spent.

HALIFAX: Enrich Hitler so that he will release the Jews?

JOE KENNEDY: Money is the universal language, Lord Halifax. Money will make this plan work.

CHAMBERLAIN: Who will supply the money, Joe?

JOE KENNEDY: Your government will invest in this program; the French; my own government will put up funds; and there will be large private contributions from the United States. The cost will be dwarfed by the savings.

HALIFAX: The Kennedy Plan.

JOE KENNEDY: There is not a moment to lose. We are going to have to press on this.

HALIFAX: How many Jews will the United States accept?

JOE KENNEDY: Don't worry about that. I need some time to reason with both the politicians and the Zionists.

CHAMBERLAIN: I'm afraid the Zionists won't like this much. They want all the Jews to go to Palestine.

JOE KENNEDY: I understand that, but they will quickly see that Jews who have made it to Venezuela or Alaska will have the choice to later immigrate to Palestine. More work will need to be done in Palestine for that to work. In the meantime, the Jews will be allowed to leave Germany, the Germans will make money, Hitler will be happy, and war will be averted. It is not a perfect plan. There will be critics, but this plan will work, and we need to start moving on it right now.

Scene 5

Secretary of State Cordell Hull sits in his office looking at a stack of newspapers as Assistant Secretary J. P. Moffat paces around him smoking a pipe.

HULL: He is a master of public relations. A master!

MOFFAT: "The Kennedy Plan." Why do all the papers label it as the Kennedy Plan?

HULL: It's that editor Arthur Krock. Krock runs the Times foreign desk but he is on the Kennedy payroll.

MOFFAT: Is that legal? Can Joe pay an editor of the New York Times?

HULL: I suppose he's a consultant or something. Krock is supposed to keep Joe out of trouble.

MOFFAT: He's going to earn his pay on this one. Myron Taylor is going to be mad as hell about this.

HULL: Wouldn't you be? Taylor has been working for 6 months on plans to get the Jews out of Germany. He's considered all kinds of possibilities, but Joe Kennedy discovers that it's the right thing to do and suddenly it becomes the Kennedy Plan.

MOFFAT: And George Rublee is going to be upset. He's worked as hard as Taylor.

HULL: Maybe Kennedy has treed himself on this one though.

MOFFAT: How so?

HULL: The reason the President hasn't endorsed any plan is that the Zionists are insisting that the Jews go to Palestine.

MOFFAT: You think Kennedy is going to have trouble with the Zionists on this?

HULL: They'll be calling for his resignation, sure as hell.

MOFFAT: For trying to save the Jews of Germany?

HULL: Joe should have realized that he was picking up a political football that no one can handle.

MOFFAT: The Kennedy Plan. I suppose if it works out, he'll be a big hero.

HULL: Works out? That's the reason no progress has been made. The only Jews with a strong organization are the Zionists and the Zionists are only going to be happy if the Jews go to Palestine.

MOFFAT: Joe's point is that they need to get out of Germany now. They can go to Palestine later if they want.

HULL: That won't please the Zionists.

MOFFAT: Surely the Zionists can't expect the British to force the people of Palestine off from their lands.

HULL: You don't think so?

MOFFAT: Why would the British do that?

HULL: The Zionists expect the British to evict the Arabs.

MOFFAT: I can't believe that. I'm sure the Zionists will realize that something else must be done in the short term.

HULL: We'll see. No one wants to give up anything here. The Germans want the Jews out of Germany and now Austria, the Zionists want them to go to Palestine, but the people in Palestine don't want to give up their land.

MOFFAT: So maybe it should be called the Kennedy Plan.

HULL: I suppose the President could order increased Jewish immigration here. He could use an Executive Order.

MOFFAT: I wonder what the voters will say.

HULL: Or, he could take over the British Mandate in Palestine. He could use American soldiers to go over there and evict the Arabs.

MOFFAT: Americans are never going to believe that the people in Palestine seek world domination. They fell for that line in the last war.

HULL: Right and asking American soldiers to force Arabs from their homes would put a different light on 1940. We have an election to face.

MOFFAT: What should the President say? We're going to have to provide him with a statement. Does he support the Kennedy Plan or not?

HULL: I think the President will let Joe run with this one and Joe will get a little taste of politics. Education can be expensive.

Scene 6

British Ambassador RONALD LINDSAY meets with United States Assistant Secretary of State Sumner Wells in Washington, D.C.

LINDSAY: The Prime Minister and Lord Halifax have met with the Cabinet concerning Ambassador Kennedy's proposal.

WELLS: Which proposal was that?

LINDSAY: Ambassador Kennedy has pointed out the obvious humanitarian crisis going on in Germany and proposed the His

Majesty's Government take the lead in facilitating Jewish emigration from Germany.

WELLS: We have discussed several proposals.

LINDSAY: The question posed to the government was how many Jews the United Kingdom could accept now.

WELLS: How many Jews could enter the United Kingdom?

LINDSAY: That's right. Ambassador Kennedy believes that we should make inquiries to see where Jews would be accepted.

WELLS: How many Jews would the United Kingdom be able to take in the next year?

LINDSAY: What we would like to propose is that we use the quota set aside for immigration into the United States-- approximately 60,000 British citizens per year—for the Jews coming out of Europe.

(There is a long pause between Wells and the British Ambassador Ronald Lindsay.)

WELLS: That quota was specifically for British citizens.

LINDSAY: We understand that. As Ambassador Kennedy points out, these are not ordinary times and we are faced with a humanitarian crisis. The British government appreciates Ambassador Kennedy's urging for action but wishes to know what the American government is willing to do.

WELLS: The quota for immigration into the United States was intended for British citizens, not for refugees from Europe.

LINDSAY: That's right.

WELLS: We could not change the intent of the Congress in establishing this quota. It would require an Act of Congress.

LINDSAY: How many Jews would the United States be willing to accept this year?

WELLS: That question will need to be addressed by the President and the Congress. It is not yet something which has been debated.

LINDSAY: Surely, Ambassador Kennedy is asking these questions on the direction of the President. If the United States is asking other countries how many Jews they will accept in this humanitarian crisis, that question must have been addressed by your government.

WELLS: I will need to ask the Ambassador exactly on whose direction he is working.

LINDSAY: This is a terribly important issue. We are not disputing either the depth of the crisis or the need for rapid response, but we will need to understand the nature of the American proposal.

WELLS: Yes, of course, and that is being formulated now.

Scene 7

Newspapermen question President Roosevelt at a press conference.

ROOSEVELT: The unemployment rate will soon start to drop once again. Every economic recovery experiences good months and bad months. While we've had a little bump here, I am confident that our overall recovery is intact. More jobs are on the way.

REPORTER: Mr. President, if we increase the number of men looking for jobs, and the economy only creates so many jobs, will the unemployment rate go up if more men enter the United States?

ROOSEVELT: That makes sense, sure, but overall, the unemployment rate is going down. We've only had a little bump.

REPORTER: We hear from Europe that Ambassador Kennedy is proposing that countries around the world ready themselves to accept a great influx of Jewish immigrants.

ROOSEVELT: There are some significant problems, as you know, in Germany and Austria.

REPORTER: Will the German Jews immigrate into the United States?

ROOSEVELT: No plans have been made yet to change our immigration quotas.

REPORTER: The Kennedy Plan, as the papers are referring to it, means that all countries will need to take refugees from Europe.

ROOSEVELT: I have not been told about the Kennedy plan.

REPORTER: Would refugees make the unemployment rate even higher?

ROOSEVELT: I can't comment on this "because I know nothing of what has been happening in London."

Scene 8

With telephones in hand, Secretary of State Cordell Hull stands on one side of the stage while Ambassador Kennedy stands on the other.

HULL: What plan have you proposed to the British?

JOE KENNEDY: Nothing formal yet. What I did do was have a conversation with Malcolm MacDonald-- the Colonial Secretary-- over lunch. We talked about many things, but I pointed out that the British have so many colonies and mandates that they should designate some land to help resolve this humanitarian refugee problem in Europe.

HULL: And how was your request received, Joe?

JOE KENNEDY: Well, MacDonald said that the British were very sympathetic to the Jews who want to leave Germany and I said that the world was hearing a lot about sympathy but wasn't seeing any action on this problem. Somebody should move on this. Everyone is sympathetic but the time to act is now.

HULL: What did you propose?

JOE KENNEDY: Again, I didn't propose anything. I merely pointed out that if the British would designate an area in Africa say, or anywhere else for that matter, it would be possible to raise funds to get this process started.

HULL: The Kennedy Plan.

JOE KENNEDY: That is the way the idea has been labeled in the press.

HULL: You know Myron Taylor and George Rublee have been working on this plan for months.

JOE KENNEDY: I know that ideas like this have been kicked around, yes. Maybe you should call it the Taylor Plan. Let's get it done.

HULL: The President does not believe that we have the political support in the United States to accept a large immigration of Jews or any other refugees now and the Congress will want to be heard.

JOE KENNEDY: Given the circumstances, he could use an Executive Order to change the quotas. We don't have a lot of time for public hearings.

HULL: Joe, you can't just tell the British what their government should do; you don't even know what your own government is willing or able to do.

JOE KENNEDY: What? Why did you guys send me over here if it wasn't to look for ways to solve this problem? If we don't come up with a solution here, and I mean soon, this situation is going to fall apart.

HULL: What do you mean fall apart?

JOE KENNEDY: Well, anyone can see that Hitler is pushing the Jews out of Germany. That Jewish kid killed a Nazi officer in Paris and the Nazis answered with an attack on Jewish property throughout Germany. That night of broken glass was not a simple mistake-- it was meant as a clear signal that Jews are no longer welcome in Germany.

HULL: We're aware of that.

JOE KENNEDY: The Zionists have a deal to move Jews from Germany to Palestine, but it isn't happening fast enough. The people in Palestine can't handle more Jews immediately. That will take time. We need to figure out a way to move them to other areas and if we don't, the consequences will be extreme.

HULL: What consequences?

JOE KENNEDY: You know this, Cordell. Some of the Jews in the United States criticize any effort to normalize relations with the Germans. If we can't talk to them, if we isolate them economically and can't discuss any solutions, war will become inevitable. It is either peace or war, Cordell, and I am here to work for peace.

HULL: Joe, as an ambassador, you speak for the government of the United States. When you push the Colonial Secretary to designate a territory for Jewish immigration, it has the same force as if the President was pushing him.

JOE KENNEDY: This problem is very real, Cordell. Somebody has got to start pushing.

HULL: You can't make such comments without the approval of the State Department and we can't give you approval without authorization from the President and the Congress. You are on some very unstable ground.

JOE KENNEDY: (angry) God damn it, Cordell, that's the reason I'm here. You guys can't criticize the Kennedy Plan in one breath and then say you came up with it first in the next. You can't have it both ways. Now, let's not back away from this. We can solve the entire problem; we can avert a war, by showing that we want to help the German Jews emigrate to safety.

HULL: They shouldn't be forced to emigrate, Joe.

JOE KENNEDY: I am not debating that. I'm only saying that Hitler wants them out of there and we need to work with him, not isolate and antagonize him. We can't change the government in Germany. We can only show good faith and set up a program to get the refugees out. Otherwise, we will slip into a war.

HULL: Joe, you know we've been friends for many years but I'm speaking for the Department of State now and for the President of the United States: you can't simply push your own ideas as if they were laws passed by the Congress. We're a government.

JOE KENNEDY: This is a great opportunity. We can show Hitler that we want to work with him to allow emigration from Germany. He'll soon realize that the Jews are too important to his economy and declare that he won't allow any more of them to emigrate. The whole tone of things will change.

HULL: Tell me that you understand that you can't just make proposals and sell them to foreign governments?

JOE KENNEDY: Of course, I understand that, but somebody has got to take some risk here and get this process moving.

HULL: The boss wants to slow things down there. That's all. Tell me that you understand.

JOE KENNEDY: I understand that's the government's position. I don't agree, but I understand.

Scene 9

President Roosevelt and Secretary of State Cordell Hull receive Joseph Kennedy in the Oval Office in December 1938.

ROOSEVELT: I didn't say that I didn't support you. I said that I would have to be briefed on the plan. You have always had my full support.

JOE KENNEDY: How can we have peaceful resolution if I'm criticized every time I try to establish discussion with the Germans? I propose that we try to find areas of common interest; I'm attacked. I propose that we try to find places for the German Jews to go; I'm attacked. Tell me what I should be doing?

ROOSEVELT: You're doing a good job there, Joe.

HULL: We can't have you telling the British that the refugee problem is their problem.

JOE KENNEDY: I never said that. I'm only saying that we need to get started on it. We need to decide where they are going to go and make a deal with Hitler to pay the costs of transporting them there.

ROOSEVELT: (calling out to his secretary) Where is Henry? I asked Secretary Morgenthau to join us. I wonder where he is.

JOE KENNEDY: There will be objections. I'm sure that the newspapers in England and here will say that we are rewarding Hitler for his aggressive policies, but if we are thinking of the population trapped under his control, what choice do we have but to make a deal with him?

HULL: Joe, I can't tell you how complicated this issue is for the President. No matter what we do, we face tremendous criticism.

JOE KENNEDY: I believe that is how the Prime Minister feels. He is being hounded in the British press because he avoided a war over Czechoslovakia.

ROOSEVELT: I invited Henry to join us because I want you to hear some of his thoughts, Joe.

JOE KENNEDY: You should remember Mr. President that the British made a deal over the Sudetenland because they had not rearmed. They still have not rearmed. We do not have the guns and planes to fight a war with Germany right now. What choice did Chamberlain have?

ROOSEVELT: The papers here are starting to say that he should have fought.

JOE KENNEDY: Let me guess: Walter Lippmann over at the New Republic? Do you think those columnists have more information than we do?

ROOSEVELT: I don't know. I know he's very influential.

JOE KENNEDY: The British are still in no position to defend themselves. We were unwilling to join with the British in the defense of the Sudetenland. What are we going to say when it comes to Poland?

MORGENTHAU: (entering) We must draw the line somewhere. Better to fight them in Europe than fight them here.

ROOSEVELT: Good day, Henry.

MORGENTHAU: The Nazis are a threat to our national security. They must be stopped.

JOE KENNEDY: Why do you say that they are a threat to our national security, Henry?

MORGENTHAU: Hitler will never be satisfied. Any deal we make with him will be broken.

JOE KENNEDY: How are you able to predict the future? How do you know what Hitler will accept?

MORGENTHAU: There is no reasoning with Hitler. The atrocities that are leaking out of Germany require we stand up to him now.

JOE KENNEDY: How do you know there is no reasoning with him with if we don't try?

MORGENTHAU: His treatment of Germany's religious minorities is deplorable.

JOE KENNEDY: We all agree on that but starting a war will only hurt them.

MORGENTHAU: We should just get someone in there and shoot him.

JOE KENNEDY: Isn't that what caused this last assault on the Jews? A Jewish kid in Paris killed a Nazi officer and the Nazis responded by looting synagogues throughout Germany.

MORGENTHAU: Are you defending the Nazis?

JOE KENNEDY: Far from it. I'm trying to think of the Jews still trapped in Germany and Austria and all the innocent people of Europe. How will all your aggressiveness affect them?

MORGENTHAU: If the British would open Palestine, the Jews would have a place to go.

JOE KENNEDY: Exactly, but they can't without moving Arabs off from their land by gunpoint. Would you support that?

MORGENTHAU: It is what they promised.

JOE KENNEDY: Who promised?

MORGENTHAU: The British promised to establish a Jewish homeland.

JOE KENNEDY: Would you support that? What gives the British the right to push the Palestinians off from their land-- under any circumstances?

MORGENTHAU: That was the Balfour Declaration.

JOE KENNEDY: No, it wasn't. The Balfour Declaration specifically guaranteed the rights of the existing people in Palestine. The British can't force the Arabs off from land that they have occupied for the last 18 centuries. Are we willing to do that?

HULL: The Neutrality Acts don't allow us to do much of anything in Europe-- certainly not invade Palestine.

ROOSEVELT: Now, gentlemen, I only bring you together to appreciate that there are differences of opinion in this very administration. Joe is just observing the obvious: Hitler wants the Jews out of Germany.

MORGENTHAU: They should be allowed to go to Palestine.

JOE KENNEDY: Henry, I can promise you that the British are not going to point guns at people and force them out of their homes, whether Arabs or any other population. If the British feel like a war is possible, and how could they think anything else, the last thing they would do is antagonize the people who supply them with oil.

MORGENTHAU: To suggest that we move the Jews of Europe to South America or Africa is to abandon the Balfour Declaration.

JOE KENNEDY: The Balfour Declaration was just that: a declaration. It wasn't a law or a treaty-- it was the declaration of a goal. No one asked the people in Palestine if the British could give away their land.

HULL: Either way, this is not our fight. Americans don't want to send our sons to settle a European dispute.

MORGENTHAU: It could become our fight, Cordell.

ROOSEVELT: Thank you, gentlemen. Maybe you could excuse us for just a few minutes. I haven't seen Joe for several months and I want to have a private chat.

(Morgenthau and Hull leave.)

ROOSEVELT: I think you see that opinion is not uniform here, Joe.

JOE KENNEDY: The Secretary of State wants to stay out and Secretary of the Treasury is calling for a war with Germany.

ROOSEVELT: I'm the president but I'm only a politician. I only have power while I hold this office. If this question were put to the voters, I can assure you that neutrality would be confirmed. This country has no interest in fighting a war in Europe or Palestine. So, I can't beat the drum for war unless I want to lose in 1940. Then we would have a government which would guarantee isolationism.

JOE KENNEDY: We should prepare ourselves. Whatever U boats we need to develop, whatever tanks or fighter planes we need to work on, we better get started.

ROOSEVELT: I agree completely. That's the reason I need people with your insight working for me in London.

JOE KENNEDY: Every newspaper repeats the rumor that I've fallen from your good graces.

ROOSEVELT: All nonsense. You have my complete confidence.

JOE KENNEDY: Mr. President, I'm going down to Florida to think over whether I can continue to be effective in London if the press constantly undermines me. They won't miss me in London, but I would like for you to give my idea some thought. If we can defuse the Jewish refugee question, we can prevent a war in Europe-- and that would save many lives.

ROOSEVELT: Joe, I couldn't do this job without men of your courage. Don't get too far away from your telephone. Things might change here or in London and you may need to get back quickly.

JOE KENNEDY: I continue to serve, Mr. President.

Scene 10

Foreign Minister Lord Halifax and Prime Minister Chamberlain meet on 10 Downing Street in March 1939.

HALIFAX: No shots were fired.

CHAMBERLAIN: (a pause) They gave up without a fight.

HALIFAX: The reports are that Herr Hitler entered Prague the day after the capitulation; but rather than coming in after a column of tanks, he entered in a motorcade of Mercedes limousines.

CHAMBERLAIN: Our loan of twelve million pounds has been lost.

HALIFAX: (Walks over and looks out a window.) Yes, I suppose that the money has been lost as well as the city. Czechoslovakia has been renamed. It is now the Protectorate of Monrovia and Slovenia--so Hitler proclaimed from Prague Castle.

(The men stand and sit in stunned silence.)

CHAMBERLAIN: Czechoslovakia has fallen without a battle. It is hard to imagine.

HALIFAX: Not really. The Czechs had no modern army. Had they resisted, they would have been blown to bits. The question is what can be done to contain this evil man.

CHAMBERLAIN: It is difficult for us to argue that he is a war monger since the election in the Sudetenland showed 97% in favor of the Nazis.

HALIFAX: An election no doubt as fair as the one conducted by the Nazis in Austria.

CHAMBERLAIN: To enter Prague with the permission of the Czech government hardly portrays Hitler as an aggressor; still, if we want to continue to rule this government, we are going to have to announce a plan to contain him.

HALIFAX: The Poles have already approached us for a loan. We are going to have to decide what we can do to help them.

CHAMBERLAIN: It is such a frustration. We are close to a peace.

HALIFAX: We are very close. With Danzig and the Polish Corridor, Hitler will have delivered on everything he promised Germany: he will have restored the German nation.

CHAMBERLAIN: If only we could negotiate the matter in Poland, we could rightfully claim that we had defused a disaster.

HALIFAX: Yes, but the fact that Herr Hitler has behaved so aggressively makes me believe that we will face tremendous pressure to confront him.

CHAMBERLAIN: We will, no doubt, we will.

HALIFAX: The Poles would like a loan of 60 million pounds to rearm.

CHAMBERLAIN: We need to re-arm ourselves. How can we offer protection to Poland?

HALIFAX: We can not. We lack either a powerful air force or an army that could possibly defend Poland.

CHAMBERLAIN: Does it make sense to loan them money for new arms?

HALIFAX: Might the Nazis see such a loan as a provocative? Are they likely to watch as the Poles re-arm?

CHAMBERLAIN: Perhaps we should simply announce our commitment to protect Poland. That way, the Nazis will know that if they attack Poland, they will have a war with Britain.

HALIFAX: Imagine for a moment what our position would be if he did go into Poland. We do not have the air power to strike Berlin. We do not have an army to engage the Wehrmacht. I've worried whether we have adequate defenses to protect the French.

CHAMBERLAIN: Let's not get ahead of ourselves. Hitler is not going to simply roll over the French.

CHAMBERLAIN: The only thing remaining on his list of promises is the restoration of Danzig into the Reich. Why not? It is a German city. They are waving Nazi flags in Danzig. Why should we oppose him?

HALIFAX: We agree that Danzig can go to Germany. We have always agreed on that. It was German territory before the war. How do we get the Poles to make a deal with the Germans?

CHAMBERLAIN: Surely, they will appreciate their own situation. They can't think that they could hold off a German invasion and they can't think that we could possibly save them from this island.

HALIFAX: It is just his threatening manner. His aggressiveness frightens his neighbors.

CHAMBERLAIN: He has not yet fired a shot. He's been aggressive, but he has not used his new military to conquer any nation.

HALIFAX: You are right. We are very close to being done with this. If we can get Danzig back into Germany, we can avoid all the loss of life a war would mean.

CHAMBERLAIN: I believe that we need to continue to negotiate but we are not going to have the leadership much longer if we do not draw the line.

HALIFAX: Must we guarantee the sovereignty of Poland?

CHAMBERLAIN: I think so.

HALIFAX: If we guarantee Poland, we will give the Polish government time and the power to negotiate with the Germans

CHAMBERLAIN: The Germans must understand that if they make moves without a treaty, they will face war from the western allies. It is that simple.

HALIFAX: There was so much death from the last war. What did we gain from it all?

CHAMBERLAIN: We lost an entire generation of Englishmen--

HALIFAX: --and they lost an entire generation of Germans, to say nothing of the losses in France and the massive slaughter that has taken place in Russia.

CHAMBERLAIN: How much better the world would be today if the government had negotiated a reasonable peace in the last war. There was no reason to starve people in Germany. It was horrible and cruel.

HALIFAX: And given us the disaster we face today.

CHAMBERLAIN: I remain committed to peace, but I think we must guarantee Poland. Otherwise, we will look like a couple of harmless old men. We acted like reasonable men at Munich, but Hitler took what we agreed upon and has now taken more. We must clearly communicate to him that rules must be followed, or war will be inevitable.

Scene 11

Former Associate Justice LOUIS BRANDEIS and Rabbi SOLOMON GOLDMAN wait in the White House for a meeting with President Roosevelt in May 1939.

BRANDEIS: We've got to get this turned around.

GOLDMAN: You should remember that without American support, the British are going to be in trouble, big trouble.

BRANDEIS: That's the reason we're here. If the President will give Chamberlain a call, we might get the restrictions suspended.

GOLDMAN: What is the most recent report?

BRANDEIS: Unless we make some headway, the British will recommend that Jewish immigration be restricted and that within ten years, Palestine will become a free state--with an Arab majority.

GOLDMAN: That's an outrage. We've got to do something.

(A steward wheels the president into the room. Both Rabbi Goldman and Brandeis stand.)

BRANDEIS and GOLDMAN: Mr. President.

ROOSEVELT: (shaking hands) Rabbi. Louie. What's the news from London?

BRANDEIS: That's the reason we're here today, Mr. President.

ROOSEVELT: And?

BRANDEIS: The news isn't good. The word is that the British will propose further restrictions on Jewish immigration.

GOLDMAN: This at a time when Jews desperately need to get out of Germany.

(Brandeis quietly waves his hand to signal Goldman that he will make the arguments.)

BRANDEIS: Mr. President, the concern is that if we decide to make a deal with Hitler, there won't be anywhere for the German Jews to go.

ROOSEVELT: I've heard that there is already a deal with Hitler to allow Jews to get to Palestine.

BRANDEIS: Many Jews have made it out, yes. We think that the Jews of Germany should go to Palestine. A great new nation of Jews will be created.

ROOSEVELT: There is already a nation of people there, Louie, and my understanding is that they don't want to leave.

BRANDEIS: We need to get them out of there, Mr. President.

ROOSEVELT: How do you propose that we do that?

BRANDEIS: We're only talking about two or three hundred thousand people. If we can move those Arabs to Syria or Iraq, we will be able to re-settle the Jews into their God given homeland.

ROOSEVELT: That's some very contested real estate.

BRANDEIS: Money does wonderful things, Mr. President. I think we can raise some money to help relocate that Arab population.

ROOSEVELT: Do you see the United States and Britain contributing to the fund?

BRANDEIS: If the Jewish community can put together $100 million, do you think that the Americans and the British could also put up $100 million each?

ROOSEVELT: I think so. Yes. I think that would be an excellent idea.

BRANDEIS: I think $300 million would go a long way in that part of the world, Mr. President.

ROOSEVELT: What if those Arabs don't want to sell their property?

BRANDEIS: They're going to have to be moved off that land, Mr. President.

ROOSEVELT: Moved off the land?

BRANDEIS: That's why we're going to pay them. We're going to buy the land with the relocation money. Some will go to the Arab property owners, some will go to the Germans for helping with the re-location, some will need to be used for building homes.

ROOSEVELT: You gentlemen need to correct me, but my understanding is that the Arabs are resisting Jewish purchases of their land.

BRANDEIS: We don't have a lot of time here, Mr. President. Hitler is not a stable man. We need to get those people out as soon as possible.

ROOSEVELT: I appreciate that, but I can't direct American soldiers to force Arabs out of their homes.

BRANDEIS: That's the reason we need the British to clear that land.

ROOSEVELT: Look, Louie, the British are not going to move people at gunpoint. No respectable country wants to move people off their land by gunpoint.

BRANDEIS: If we can open up Palestine, we can help Chancellor Hitler realize his goal of getting the Jews out of Germany.

ROOSEVELT: Is it practical to ask the British to move the Arabs? Can they really attack the peaceful Arab population in Palestine?

BRANDEIS: Mr. President, the Jews have been big supporters of the New Deal.

ROOSEVELT: They certainly have been.

BRANDEIS: We need 200 or 300 thousand Arabs to go to Iraq.

ROOSEVELT: "I'll work on the project myself when I get a little time" but you must know that the American people aren't going to want to send their sons off to settle European problems.

GOLDMAN: We know we have a great friend in the White House.

ROOSEVELT: It is not a question of sympathy, my friends; it is only a question of whether we have the time and opportunity.

BRANDEIS: That's right. No one knows what Hitler might do next.

GOLDMAN: All the more reason to open Palestine!

Scene 12

General Motors business executive JAMES MOONEY returns to the embassy to see Ambassador Kennedy in May 1939.

JOE KENNEDY: Let me read to you what I wrote to Undersecretary Sumner Wells: "I met this morning with James Mooney who oversees General Motors Export business and head of the German plant. He invited me to dine with him in Paris Saturday night.

Another party at the dinner will be a personal friend of Hitler and high in influence at the Reichsbank...This man is in the inner circle, from what Mooney said....Is there any particular information regarding financial and political matters which you would like me to try to obtain?"

MOONEY: Good, Joe.   That sounds like you asked the right question.

JOE KENNEDY: Not so good. Listen to what Sumner sent back: "I have talked over your message with the Secretary and we both feel very strongly that at this particular time it would be almost impossible to prevent your trip to Paris and the names of the persons you will see in Paris from being given a great deal of publicity. If an erroneous impression in the press here were given regarding your conference with this individual from Germany it would inevitably create speculation and unfortunate comment...I hope you will not undertake this trip at the moment."

MOONEY: That's incredible. They are so worried about a bad headline, they won't let you even talk to Goering's finance guy?

JOE KENNEDY: It is hard to believe, but they must be careful with the press in New York and Washington.

MOONEY: It would be unpardonable to cancel the meeting. The Germans will be very disappointed.

JOE KENNEDY: I can only do what they will let me do, Jim.

MOONEY: This could be a feeler for something much bigger. The National Socialists are hemmed in and they know it. It is either make trade or make war. They are reaching out to see if trade is possible.

JOE KENNEDY: Well, I suppose I could call the President and see if he'll let me do it.

MOONEY: If the press won't even let ambassadors talk to the Germans, if the government itself is so sensitive to the press that it can't have discussions, what hope is there for peace?

JOE KENNEDY: Before you call it off, let me see if I can sell it to the boss. Call me in the morning and I'll tell you what he said. In the meantime, make sure that this doesn't leak out.

Scene 13

Secretary of the Treasury Henry Morgenthau, Jr. stands with Sumner Wells and Secretary Hull around President Roosevelt's wheelchair in the White House.

HULL: Sumner told Kennedy he shouldn't meet with him.

MORGENTHAU: The very idea of it is an outrage. It shows that Kennedy can't be trusted.

HULL: He asked permission, Henry. He followed the rules.

MORGENTHAU: He should know that to meet with representatives of the high command would look like we are willing to talk to them.

HULL: We are willing to talk. The President sent a letter to the dictators inviting discussion about peace.

MORGENTHAU: Peace with Hitler is impossible.

HULL: It is impossible if we don't allow any discussions. Besides the publicity of the meeting, I don't see much harm in it.

MORGENTHAU: You don't see the harm in talking with murderers?

HULL: Keep in mind that there are Arabs in Palestine who are claiming that Palestinians are being murdered and pushed off their land by Jews.

MORGENTHAU: Not a reasonable comparison!

HULL: I just think we need to remember that discussions are the best tools of diplomacy.

ROOSEVELT: Gentlemen, I think it might be appropriate to have discussions with representatives of Germany. I have no problem with that. We should start somewhere.

(Secretary enters the meeting.)

SECRETARY: Mr. President, Ambassador Kennedy has called again. He wishes to speak to you personally.

MORGENTHAU: This is unacceptable. Are we going to dignify the German government with discussions?

HULL: How else can we avoid a war, Henry?

MORGENTHAU: We must keep the pressure of the boycott on until the German government crumbles from within.

ROOSEVELT: Tell Joe that I'm busy right now. I'll call him back in a few minutes.

HULL: The German government is a dictatorship. If men don't volunteer for the army, they are taken out in the street and shot. Is it reasonable to think that civilians can overthrow that kind of government?

ROOSEVELT: Henry, did you read my letter to Chancellor Hitler?

MORGENTHAU: Yes, Mr. President.

ROOSEVELT: Surely you saw that I agreed to enter trade negotiations if the Germans agree to commit themselves to peace.

MORGENTHAU: Which they have not done.

ROOSEVELT: They say they are committed to peace. Remember, Henry, the Germans have not fired a single bullet. They annexed Austria without a fight and Hitler bargained his way into Prague. There hasn't been a major battle with Germany since 1918.

HULL: It might be that the Germans are sending a peace party to meet with Kennedy. He would be the one they might approach.

MORGENTHAU: That would be a terrible disaster—it would send the wrong signal.

HULL: How so? Having discussions in Paris is not the same as waving a white flag. We are not announcing the end of the boycott. We're just allowing Kennedy to talk to the Germans.

MORGENTHAU: A representative of Hermann Goering.

ROOSEVELT: Cordell, I'd like you to call Joe and tell him that I don't feel comfortable with him going to Paris. We don't want the French to start negotiations with Hitler; so, we shouldn't signal that we are having talks. Henry is right-- Joe gets a lot of publicity. Maybe we can open some discussions that are a bit less public.

Scene 14

Hermann Goering's chief economist Dr. HELMUTH WOHLTHAT stands as Ambassador Joseph Kennedy enters Wohlthat's hotel room in London on May 8, 1939. They shake hands.

JOE KENNEDY: I'm sorry to meet you under these circumstances but my government is very concerned with how our press might react.

WOHLTHAT: Of course, I understand.

JOE KENNEDY: I believe that we can avoid a war.

WOHLTHAT: As do I, Mr. Ambassador.

JOE KENNEDY: I can see that some mistakes were made during the last war. That's the reason Prime Minister Chamberlain has pushed to make amends.

WOHLTHAT: Wasn't Mr. Churchill himself quoted as saying that if Americans hadn't entered the war there would have been no Russian Revolution, no German Revolution, no rise of the National Socialists?

JOE KENNEDY: My understanding is that he has denied saying that.

WOHLTHAT: He was quoted as saying it. Now he is trying to prompt the Americans into another war.

JOE KENNEDY: Still, Dr. Wohlthat, we are not debating what happened in the last war.

WOHLTHAT: No, but you asked why Chancellor Hitler is angry with the Jewish citizens. The international Jewish community declared war on Germany in 1933. They declared a trade boycott when the National Socialists took office and now they are agitating for another full-scale war.

JOE KENNEDY: Chancellor Hitler recently declared that if the Jews involve Germany in another international war, he will exterminate the Jews of Europe. That's not language which will promote a reconciliation.

WOHLTHAT: What should we do if the Jewish financiers arrange another war of starvation against Germany? Should we see that our Jews are served their food first?

JOE KENNEDY: I can understand why there is anger over the last war, and I can see why Hitler believes he can use his new military to re-unite the German people. He must understand that in its chaos war becomes unpredictable. The German people will be better served by peace.

WOHLTHAT: That's the reason I am here today Ambassador Kennedy. At the direction of the German Chancellor, I was to meet with you in Paris. When your government forbade that, the Fuhrer allowed me to come to London. Hitler wants a peaceful solution.

JOE KENNEDY: Then why does he threaten the Polish border?

WOHLTHAT: Those lands were German before the last war. German people live in those lands now. If Hitler is confronted with abuse of German citizens in cities which were once German, his instinct is to protect them. Any national leader would have such an instinct.

JOE KENNEDY: He should not act with an army. He should seek negotiations.

WOHLTHAT: Which is what I am doing right now. The international economies continue the Jewish-led boycott; they isolate us; they assassinate our officers in foreign capitals; they try to prevent diplomatic discussions; they agitate for war. If we could trade, we could continue to make progress with peaceful adjustments. If we are not allowed to trade, and at present we are not, what choice does Germany have?

JOE KENNEDY: Our job is to see that this war gets called off before it gets started. I stand with the advocates of peace.

Scene 15

Rose Kennedy shows her daughter Rosemary the proper way to set the table for a family dinner in Southern France in August 1939.

ROSE: The sharp part of the knife is always placed to the inside so that it faces the plate.

ROSEMARY: Like this?

ROSE: That's right, dear, and then the salad fork goes to the outside of the dinner fork.

(Rosemary places the utensils next to the plates. Joseph Kennedy talks with his sons Joe Jr. and Jack on some nearby patio chairs. Kick Kennedy enters and reaches out to mess up Jack's hair as she walks toward the table. JFK flashes a smile at his sister as she walks by. Kick pauses by the table to look at her older sister Rosemary set the table.)

ROSE: That's very nice, Rosemary.

KICK: Nice, but the spoon should be further out.

(Rosemary straightens up as if stricken.)

ROSEMARY: The spoon what?

ROSE: Kick, you go back and sit down with your brothers. Rosemary and I are setting the table. Everyone should know how to set a proper table.

ROSEMARY: What's wrong with the spoon?!

ROSE: There is nothing wrong with the spoon, dear.

ROSEMARY: (loudly at Kick) There's nothing wrong with the spoon.

KICK: No, there isn't. That's a very good job, Rosemary.

ROSEMARY: Why does Kick always say mean things to me?

ROSE: This is none of Kick's concern, dear. This is our project.

ROSEMARY: (To Kick) This is our project!

(Kick walks back toward her brothers while Rosemary stares at the table setting.)

ROSE: You have set a lovely table, Rosemary.

(Rosemary continues to stare at the table setting and then violently swipes plates, glasses, and silverware off from the table.)

ROSEMARY: Why do I have to set the table? Kick never sets the table.

(Two attendants stand up and move closer to Rosemary.)

ROSE: We all do what we can to help the family, Rosemary.

ROSEMARY: Kick always goes off with her boyfriend.

ROSE: Now, dear, let's take a walk for a few minutes to collect our feelings.

(Rose takes Rosemary's arm and walks with her away from the table. The attendants follow. The others look on in stunned silence.)

JOE KENNEDY: I don't know how we can best help Rosemary.

KICK: I'm sorry, daddy. I didn't mean to upset her.

JOE KENNEDY: I know. We all must be careful.

JACK: Do you think she will be able to live on her own?

JOE KENNEDY: I don't see how.

JOE JUNIOR: She has days when she is good.

JOE KENNEDY: We all should show as much love as we can.

JACK: Seems like last year, doesn't it? We're here looking at the French coastline while mother tries to comfort Rosemary and Chamberlain tries to comfort Hitler.

JOE KENNEDY laughs.

JOE KENNEDY: Something tells me we won't be here next year.

JOE JUNIOR: Why do you say that, Pop?

(A military attaché enters and presents Ambassador Kennedy with an envelope. Joe opens the envelope and unfolds a letter.)

JOE KENNEDY: (stands) God damn it!

(Everyone stands in the excitement.)

JOE KENNEDY: Oh my God, this is trouble.

JOE JUNIOR: What is it, Pop?

JOE KENNEDY: The Germans have just announced a treaty with those damn Russians. They have just announced a non-aggression pact. Now, there will be nothing to keep Hitler out of Poland.

JACK: A non-aggression pact doesn't sound so bad.

JOE KENNEDY: No, this is terrible. The only weapon Chamberlain had was the alliance with Russia-- that was his entire strategy for keeping the Germans out of Poland. Now the clever Germans have outflanked him.

JACK: It still doesn't mean war.

JOE KENNEDY: No, but it means that we are much closer. We don't have any leverage on Hitler now.

JOE JUNIOR: We're back to seeing what Hitler will accept.

JOE KENNEDY: He's a temperamental dictator prone to following his impulses.

JOE JUNIOR: They should give him Danzig. That shouldn't take so long.

Scene 16

Halifax and Chamberlain put down the briefing papers they have been reading.

CHAMBERLAIN: Do you like the part about promising to go back to be an artist?

HALIFAX: It is clear to me that Hitler is ready to quit. He wants is to have Danzig back under the German flag. He is saying that he wants to retire on top.

CHAMBERLAIN: He positions an army for invasion and then presses for concessions: that is not an acceptable style of negotiation.

HALIFAX: He says, "as soon as the problems of Danzig and the corridor are resolved, [he] will make us a comprehensive peace offer and limit armaments. [He] wishes to go back to peaceful pursuits and become an artist, which is what [he] always wanted to be."

CHAMBERLAIN: Touching.

HALIFAX: Well, the man got rejected from art school. English gas blinded him in the last war. Hitler believes that the world works by threat of force.

CHAMBERLAIN: He has used that political tool well so far.

(The secretary announces the arrival of Ambassador Kennedy and Lord Cadogan to the cabinet room.)

SECRETARY: Lord Cadogan and His Excellency, Ambassador Joseph Kennedy. .

(They enter and are handed the papers the Foreign Secretary and Prime Minister have been reading.)

CHAMBERLAIN: Hitler has entered negotiations.

HALIFAX: Something that must be viewed with the highest relief.

CHAMBERLAIN: He claims that he has entered the negotiations with the Poles solely out of a desire to insure his friendship with Great Britain.

HALIFAX: A flattering statement, even if meant insincerely.

JOE KENNEDY: President Roosevelt told me that Hitler has presented the Poles with 16 separate demands and he is demanding that someone with full administrative power appear in Berlin to resolve the questions within 24 hours.

CHAMBERLAIN: Hitler is acting like a petulant child.

JOE KENNEDY: He is negotiating.

HALIFAX: That's true. We are in talks. We should be grateful for that.

JOE KENNEDY: Damn grateful! Two armies are now facing each other at the border.

CADOGAN: No doubt the reason he wants immediate resolution.

JOE KENNEDY: Quite frankly, I can't imagine the delay here. The Poles must know that it is time to give the people who say they are German citizens back to Germany. How hard can this be?

CHAMBERLAIN: It isn't that the outcome will change the world much, Joe. It is the way that Hitler is demanding that it be done.

JOE KENNEDY: Allied governments delayed restoring the German state for years before the National Socialists ever took power. This whole disaster should have resolved 10 years ago. Hitler is making these armed demands because we've delayed restoring Germany.

HALIFAX: We understand his frustrations, Joe, but we can hardly be seen trying to accommodate him right now.

JOE KENNEDY: We shouldn't care how we're seen-- nobody is going to be thinking about how we're seen when German airplanes are bombing Warsaw.

CHAMBERLAIN: I don't believe that this government would sustain a vote of confidence if we are seen to be weak.

HALIFAX: The Poles are the ones who are being asked to give up territory.

JOE KENNEDY: They think that Britain will protect them, but you can't protect Poland. It was one thing when you had the assurance of the Russians that they would stay in an alliance against Germany, but that assurance has evaporated. That is what we need to consider tonight: you have no way to protect Poland.

CHAMBERLAIN: A good argument.

JOE KENNEDY: You need to step in and tell Poland that they are on their own. They must know that if the Germans unleash their war machine, the best you can do is register your sincere regret.

HALIFAX: What will the Americans do, Joe?

JOE KENNEDY: The United States is in no position to defend the Poles, either. The President has promised me he will act soon.

CHAMBERLAIN: Act how? What will he do?

JOE KENNEDY: He hasn't told me.

HALIFAX: We need to know.

JOE KENNEDY: I've told him to contact Joseph Beck. Beck knows Hitler. The big point here is that the Polish army is not a match for the German army-- not with the German Luftwaffe. We know that.

The Germans know it. The Poles think that the western powers will protect them, and they are wrong!

CHAMBERLAIN: What do you think we should do?

JOE KENNEDY: Are we willing to burn down Europe over the fate of Danzig?

CADOGAN: No one is talking about burning down Europe.

CHAMBERLAIN: Joe, we are all against war. I have made avoiding war the centerpiece of my political career. I stand for nothing else.

JOE KENNEDY: Then don't quit now. Now is the time to realize your vision: give Hitler Danzig and then send him a new set of paints; maybe an easel.

HALIFAX: If this government were to facilitate the transfer of Danzig to Germany, we would appear to be frightened of the Germans.

JOE KENNEDY: We should be frightened of the deaths a war will cause. Give them Danzig. It's a German city.

HALIFAX: Churchill would likely occupy this office within a month.

JOE KENNEDY: Yes, let him occupy the office, but there is no reason to turn to a war prime minister when there isn't a war. If we give him a peaceful world, even he will have trouble selling a war to the English people. There are fates worse than losing power in the government.

CHAMBERLAIN: We agree. We don't want a war but are obligated to do what we said we would do.

JOE KENNEDY: The situation has changed drastically since you made that commitment, Neville, and it is very important for the Poles to understand that. The peace of the world, the lives of people in faraway countries, is now under the control of a Polish politician-- a politician who doesn't want to look weak to his own people. It's time to forget about looking weak and start thinking about saving lives.

Scene 17

Joseph Kennedy, Jr. and his brother John F. Kennedy sit in their father's office at the American Embassy in London on September 1, 1939. Ambassador Kennedy enters his office and his sons stand up.

JOE KENNEDY: Has there been a settlement?

JACK: We haven't heard anything.

JOE KENNEDY: Two armies can't face each other forever in peace. They need a deal.

JOE JUNIOR: You think today will be the day?

JOE KENNEDY: I was telling Prime Minister Chamberlain last night that he needs to start a ration program-- something that will show the public that war means sacrifice. The public has no idea of the hardships which await them if war breaks out.

JOE JUNIOR: There would be more than food shortages. That would be the least of it.

(Kick Kennedy enters the Ambassador's office.)

KICK: It has started! It has started!

JOE KENNEDY: What?

KICK: We just heard it on the wireless. German planes are bombing Poland.

JOE KENNEDY: Oh, my God.

KICK: Troops have crossed the border.

JOE KENNEDY: Terrible news. This is terrible.

JACK: Do you think we'll be pulled into it, Pop?

JOE KENNEDY: Not if I have anything to say about it. This isn't America's war. It shouldn't be Britain's war either, but I suppose it is.

JOE JUNIOR: Now we're in for some real action!

JACK: It is still very early and very limited. Maybe it can be stopped.

JOE KENNEDY: Yes, maybe it can. I've got to get moving here. We're going to need to help Americans out of England.

JOE JUNIOR: How many will want to go?

JOE KENNEDY: We need to get some ships over here to evacuate under American flagged vessels.

Rose Kennedy enters the office.

ROSE: Joe, the Prime Minister is on the radio.

(Prime Minister Chamberlain speaks on the opposite side of the stage.)

CHAMBERLAIN: "This country is at war with Germany. This is a sad day for all of us, and to none is it sadder than to me. Everything that I have worked for, everything that I have hoped for, everything that I believed in during my public life, has crashed into ruins. There is only one thing left for me to do; that is, to devote what strength and powers I have to forwarding the victory of the cause for which we have to sacrifice so much. I cannot tell what part I may be allowed to play myself; I trust I may live to see the day when Hitlerism has been destroyed and a liberated Europe has been reestablished."

Act III

Scene 1

Dressed in a military uniform, King GEORGE VI talks with Ambassador Joseph Kennedy at Buckingham Palace in October 1939.

KING GEORGE: Mr. Roosevelt was a very kind host and we enjoyed our visit very much.

JOE KENNEDY: I laughed when I heard that you were served hot dogs for lunch.

KING GEORGE: Was that printed in the papers?

JOE KENNEDY: Yes. According to the report, the President's mother was terribly embarrassed.

KING GEORGE: The whole point of the trip was to show that we have a long and close cultural history with the United States.

JOE KENNEDY: In fact, it was the first visit of a British king to the former colonies. I don't believe a king had ever visited New York-- before or after the revolution.

KING GEORGE: We don't talk about that revolution anymore, do we Mr. Kennedy?

JOE KENNEDY: No, sometimes we clean up history to match the times.

KING GEORGE: You were kind to organize the visit though and we were sorry you were not there to enjoy it with us.

JOE KENNEDY: Some of my critics close to the President blocked my invitation.

KING GEORGE: I've read that Mr. Roosevelt has many close Jewish advisors.

JOE KENNEDY: He should. They have been involved since the beginning of his administration, but so have I.

KING GEORGE: Why do they criticize you?

JOE KENNEDY: Of course, individually, I am friends with almost every one of them, but as a group, I believe that they disagree with my views.

KING GEORGE: Which of your views?

JOE KENNEDY: I'm against expansion of the war.

KING GEORGE: Chamberlain took great criticism for making the agreement at Munich.

JOE KENNEDY: His mistake was not making Danzig part of that agreement: he should have reunited the Germans of the Sudetenland and the Germans of Danzig with the Reich all at once and this mess would have been resolved. I fear for the Jews under Hitler.

KING GEORGE: They've been through wars before.

JOE KENNEDY: They haven't been through a war with Hitler before. The worst thing that could possibly happen is the very thing that now looks most likely.

KING GEORGE: Another European war.

JOE KENNEDY: Exactly. I can't imagine anything worse. The Polish president thought that your government could protect him.

KING GEORGE: A grave mistake.

JOE KENNEDY: It was a terrible mistake but now we must prevent it from becoming worse.

KING GEORGE: Germany most probably will want a peace agreement in another few weeks.

JOE KENNEDY: At the time of Munich, we had nothing. It would have taken Hitler no time at all to overwhelm the western powers. We've had a year to catch up.

KING GEORGE: Are we still so vulnerable?

JOE KENNEDY: In my opinion? Yes. There was a time when the English Channel could protect England, but the Germans have built U boats and therefore the Royal Navy is not as powerful as it once was and the Luftwaffe is the best air force in the world. The time to make peace with Hitler is right now. When he offers a deal, I would take it.

KING GEORGE: Neville might be replaced.

JOE KENNEDY: That is a small price to pay for peace. Hitler conquered Poland and he did that with Russian cooperation. Poland is a big loss, but it isn't the same as losing all of Europe.

KING GEORGE: I don't think the Prime Minister will want to give him such a large victory. Hitler now occupies Czechoslovakia and Austria.

JOE KENNEDY: Would you rather try to make a deal with him after he has conquered Poland or after he has conquered France?

KING GEORGE: What makes you think he can conquer France?

JOE KENNEDY: The French don't want to fight another war with Germany. They fought the Germans in the last war and what did that accomplish?

KING GEORGE: Surely the French will fight the Germans and we do have a navy. We will use our navy and defend our shores.

JOE KENNEDY: You can't believe that the democracies could defeat the Germans and the Russians.

KING GEORGE: No, you make a good point. I never thought it was possible that the Communists in Russia would make an alliance with the Nazis.

JOE KENNEDY: If you make peace now, there is a chance that you would be required to restore the German colonies you took after the last war.

KING GEORGE: That wouldn't be a high price to pay. Do you believe that Hitler would settle for that?

JOE KENNEDY: I don't think he's even insisting on that. All he has asked for up to now is restoration of pre-war Germany.

KING GEORGE: We should agree to that.

JOE KENNEDY: That would be a great settlement for England and for France. Then we let the colonial system run its course. It will probably end in another decade or two no matter who has administrative control. I can't imagine Hitler staying in power long after he has achieved his goals of restoring Germany. I see him retiring on a high note and resuming his painting career, as he has promised he will do.

KING GEORGE: Might Hitler persist in persecuting the Jews?

JOE KENNEDY: If we could restore the peace, we could make emigration of Germany's Jews part of the European agreement.

KING GEORGE: What does President Roosevelt think?

JOE KENNEDY: Mr. Roosevelt is surrounded by interested parties and those interested parties-- some of those interested parties-- would like to stop the Nazi anti-Semitism right where it is. Contain it.

KING GEORGE: You oppose that?

JOE KENNEDY: I favor peace. I favor stopping anti-Semitism but if I were a Jew living in Germany, or now in Poland, I'd want a peace agreement so that I could get out. If you think about it that way, you can see that the Jews of Germany would vote for my plan.

KING GEORGE: You think the Jews of Europe would support you but the English Jews criticize you?

JOE KENNEDY: Some do, and some don't.

KING GEORGE: Mr. Kennedy, I'd like to ask you to see if you can persuade your president to back your peace plan. Frankly, I think you offer the best way forward. I wish the Poles would have made an agreement with the Germans but since they didn't, I think your instinct to restore the peace is the right instinct. See if Mr. Roosevelt agrees.

Scene 2

German Ambassador HERBERT VON DIRKSEN meets with Joe Kennedy at Wall Hall, the Morgan estate, near Hertfordshire in October 1939.

JOE KENNEDY: Herbert. I'm glad to see you.

VON DIRKSEN: I'm traveling under British guard to get here but I assume our conversation will be private. Soon I'll return to Germany.

JOE KENNEDY: I'm sorry to hear that, but I suppose no one sees a reason for diplomacy when a war breaks out. Should be just be opposite.

VON DIRKSEN: Chancellor Hitler wonders why the British are not seriously considering his peace proposal.

JOE KENNEDY: I have worried about that myself.

VON DIRKSEN: He never made any claims on Britain or France. He seeks only the restoration of the German state from the last war.

JOE KENNEDY: I realize that is what he has said, but I'm afraid that confidence in him has been lost.

VON DIRKSEN: Has confidence been lost because of the treaty with Czechoslovakia?

JOE KENNEDY: Hitler agreed to stay in the Sudetenland.

VON DIRKSEN: We were invited to occupy Prague. Should we have gone to the British for their approval?

JOE KENNEDY: Hitler should have respected the agreement in Munich.

VON DIRKSEN: No shots were fired. It was all by agreement between sovereign states.

JOE KENNEDY: Shots have been fired now and we should get this war stopped.

VON DIRKSEN: Do you agree that an agreement should be made?

JOE KENNEDY: I do.

VON DIRKSEN: Chancellor Hitler has repeated that he seeks a friendship with the British. He wishes to support the British Empire and he wishes to support the American Empire. In return, he asks that he be allowed to run Germany and our local sphere of influence.

JOE KENNEDY: Are you saying that Germany would only continue to hold the lands that were previously German?

VON DIRKSEN: That's the agreement, and the Russians will occupy what they consider to be theirs. The rest of Poland goes back to the Poles.

JOE KENNEDY: Negotiation always beats war.

VON DIRKSEN: I am here to invite you to come to Berlin for a meeting with the Chancellor. Chancellor Hitler believes that you are the only diplomat in London who understands that he has no intention of starting a new world war. He believes you are uniquely positioned to negotiate the peace with England.

JOE KENNEDY: Without the support of my government, I would not be able to meet with Hitler.

VON DIRKSEN: You could. You could agree to come to Berlin. Your security would be guaranteed, of course, but you might need to come as a private citizen.

JOE KENNEDY: I suppose I could resign as Ambassador and meet with Chancellor Hitler, but that would end whatever future I have in serving my government, and my sons would be finished, too.

(The two men stand and look at each other for a few moments.)

VON DIRKSEN: The Chancellor believes that if you resigned as Ambassador and met with him, you would then be able to return to the United States and proclaim that Germany has no ambitions in either Western Europe or in the Western Hemisphere. You could run for president. You could prevent the death and suffering a new war will bring.

JOE KENNEDY: I don't believe the Germans want a war with us.

VON DIRKSEN: Hitler believes that the Jews of England will push Chamberlain to fight a war with Germany and that the Jews of the United States will push Roosevelt to fight Germany as well.

JOE KENNEDY: Some of my Jewish friends support a war and some of them don't, but the President has promised me that he will not enter another European war.

VON DIRKSEN: Chancellor Hitler does not wish to have a blood war with the Jews. He only wants them to leave Germany.

JOE KENNEDY: Might he be willing to soften that position? Might he be willing to let some of Germany's Jews stay and let others leave?

VON DIRKSEN: Where will they go? Your President Roosevelt does not favor changing American immigration policies. The British don't want more Jews going there.

JOE KENNEDY: Arrangements can be made in times of peace. Do we agree on that? Arrangements can be made. Might Hitler be willing to soften his policies against the Jews if we could normalize trade relations?

VON DIRKSEN: This is the reason the Fuhrer believes that you should come to Berlin. You can find a way to compromise. Can you imagine the number of lives you would save if you could prevent another world war?

JOE KENNEDY: I'm only an ambassador.

VON DIRKSEN: Isn't this function exactly the role of ambassadors?

JOE KENNEDY: If I were attacked for being sympathetic to the Germans, my career as a diplomat would be over.

VON DIRKSEN: How many Americans would be surprised to learn that they entered the last war to fight for a Jewish homeland in Palestine?

JOE KENNEDY: That might create some difficult problems in the United States.

VON DIRKSEN: It should. I doubt Americans would like to think they had been fooled into fighting in the last war; but there is no reason to fight another war in Europe. Hitler wants peace.

JOE KENNEDY: How do we explain that to the American people?

VON DIRKSEN: You tell them the truth. You run for president and you tell the American people that Hitler is only acting to serve Germany-- as he said he would do. The Judeo-Bolsheviks staged a revolution in Russia and then tried to extend the revolution to Germany. What would happen in America if the Judeo-Bolsheviks staged a labor rally in Washington and then took control of your government?

JOE KENNEDY: Judeo-Bolsheviks? Where do you guys come up with these terms?

VON DIRKSEN: Where do we come up with these terms? Ambassador Kennedy, your American press does not report the atrocities that the revolution has brought to Russia. Does the name Yakov Swerdlow mean anything to you? He was the Judeo-Bolshevik who murdered the Tsar and his family. The Judeo-Bolsheviks executed the entire landed class of Russia. How about the name Leon Trotsky? He was the Judeo-Bolshevik who carried out the Red Terror. Priests and nuns were tortured. Dissidents were slaughtered.

JOE KENNEDY: Revolutions can be violent.

VON DIRKSEN: Indeed, they can, sir. Trotsky initiated the policy of executing soldiers' families in the Red Army if the soldiers would not serve him. I can promise you they were not Jewish families he murdered. They were Russians. Then, after the west allowed the financiers in New York to fund the revolutionaries further, they succeeded in redistributing property throughout Russia and the Ukraine. People like you were executed on the spot-- or maybe not executed but rather publicly skinned and fed to hungry rats. People were not killed for crimes, they were killed because of they owned property.

JOE KENNEDY: I can't believe this. You must remember that in the United States very few Jews support Communism.

VON DIRKSEN: Of course, you can't believe it. You've never read anything about it. Trotsky himself wrote about the Red Terror, so there is no dispute over the facts. If you were to run for president, you would be able to inform your countrymen of the dangers posed by the Judeo-Bolsheviks. Tell the farmers in your middle west about the farmers of the Ukraine. How would your farmers feel about having their land divided up among the so-called workers-- many of them migrant laborers.

JOE KENNEDY: This is nonsense. My Jewish friends are the best businessmen I know. They don't stand for expropriating the property of others. The Jews of Germany had nothing to do with the atrocities in Russia. The Jews aren't Bolsheviks.

VON DIRKSEN: Almost all the Bolsheviks are Jews.

JOE KENNEDY: Very few Jews are Bolsheviks. You are blaming all the Jews for political actions of a few.

VON DIRKSEN: Didn't the propagandists demonize the Germans to get the Americans into the last war?

JOE KENNEDY: Herbert, we need to focus on how to prevent this war from spreading.

VON DIRKSEN: Americans must understand that we mean them no harm. We want to preserve Germany for the Germans. It is easy for you to say that the Judeo-Bolsheviks do not threaten us but look what they did to the Russians: millions of people were killed. Now your Jewish Secretary Morgenthau promises to starve the German people.

JOE KENNEDY: You can't take everything Morgenthau says so seriously.

VON DIRKSEN: You must remember that the Allies starved the Germans at the end of the last war and the Fuhrer promised he won't allow Germany to starve again. If the financiers succeed in surrounding Germany and if they turn this into another world war, Hitler will annihilate the Jews of Europe.

JOE KENNEDY: We must stop this insanity right now. The Germans have made a peace offer and the Allies should take it. No good can come from Morgenthau threatening Germany and Germany threatening the Jews. This circle of threats must stop.

Scene 3

Ambassador Joseph Kennedy is in the Prime Minister's office with Chamberlain and Foreign Secretary Halifax in late November 1939.

JOE KENNEDY: The simple fact remains that the Germans conquered Poland in less than 6 weeks. The question now is whether he will turn his armies toward the west.

CHAMBERLAIN: We must be prepared to fight.

JOE KENNEDY: I believe we should take Hitler's offer of October. He says he doesn't want to fight a war with France or England. He wishes only to restore the German state to its borders before Versailles and now he has done that. Hitler took his parade in Danzig. He wants peace. I say you give it to him.

CHAMBERLAIN: We declared support for the Poles.

JOE KENNEDY: You committed to giving the Poles an opportunity to make a peace, but the British couldn't negotiate for them. You can't protect Poland, so you must compromise. You don't even have to make an agreement. Just leave Hitler alone. Figure out a way to get the Jews out of Germany and Poland. If he wants them out of there, if that is really what motivates him, fine, help them get out. That would help him, it would help the Jews, and it would keep the peace. Whatever it costs would be a bargain compared to war.

HALIFAX: The English Jews are adamant that we don't make any deal with Hitler.

JOE KENNEDY: The Jews in Palestine made a deal. They have a transfer agreement. They see the benefit.

HALIFAX: The English Jews want a change in leadership in Germany.

JOE KENNEDY: The English Jews are not in Germany or Austria. They are not the ones who are now getting confined in Poland. Hitler said in January that if the international Jewish community succeeds in turning this into another world war wherein the Germans are again starved into submission, he will exterminate the Jews of Europe. He said that.

CHAMBERLAIN: No one would ever do such a thing.

JOE KENNEDY: He's obviously a dangerous man: why test him?

HALIFAX: He's not a proper man.

JOE KENNEDY: No, he's not a proper man. He's an unstable man with a lot of power. I say you take his peace agreement and make evacuation of the Jews out of Germany part of the settlement. Everyone wins.

CHAMBERLAIN: The newspapers would have my head.

JOE KENNEDY: To hell with the newspapers. Think of the people who are in his clutches. You are the last hope for England. If you do not seek peace, no one will seek peace. If you and Lord Halifax leave the leadership, Hitler will roll over the French and invade England. With the Russians as his allies, there would be no way to stop him

HALIFAX: We can't beat Hitler alone.

JOE KENNEDY: War is not inevitable. There is still time to take his offer. You and the Prime Minister have struggled to avoid a war and I believe that you have been right. You should make a deal and avoid the further destruction of Europe.

(A secretary announces the arrival of the First Lord of the Admiralty, WINSTON CHURCHILL.)

SECRETARY: The First Lord of the Admiralty, Mr. Churchill.

CHAMBERLAIN: You've come at just the right time, Winston. The Ambassador from the United States believes we should take Hitler's peace treaty.

CHURCHILL: (shaking Kennedy's hand) How are you, Joe?

JOE KENNEDY: I'm going back to meet with President Roosevelt next week.

CHURCHILL: Good. Good. I wish we could avoid another war with the Germans. I do.

JOE KENNEDY: Then why not try?

CHURCHILL: (Churchill takes a cigar out of his pocket case and lights it.) I think we did try. We supported their occupation of the Sudetenland at Munich. The Prime Minister showed good faith there, but how was he rewarded? Hitler moved into Prague.

JOE KENNEDY: He did that with the permission of the Czechoslovakian president. The Germans didn't invade.

CHURCHILL: When Hitler occupied all of Czechoslovakia, Neville quite rightly stood on the floor of the Commons and announced that if he went into Poland, he would have a war with England.

JOE KENNEDY: The English were in no position to keep him out of Poland.

CHURCHILL: Now he will have his war with England.

JOE KENNEDY: He has no desire for a war with England. In his public speeches, he continues to insist that he will respect the sovereignty of France and England and their colonies.

CHURCHILL: What about Poland?

JOE KENNEDY: He will keep the parts of Poland which were part of Germany prior to the last war.

CHURCHILL: The Chancellor seeks a great German Empire.

JOE KENNEDY: That's not what he says—but let's say you're right. Let's say he is trying to emulate the British. I'm sure he would like to do with the Russians what England has done with India, but that doesn't mean he will do it. He might like to, but if we have a peace in place, if we can develop a community of nations designed to avoid wars, he might be constrained.

CHURCHILL: If we are going to have to fight them, why not fight them while we can beat them?

JOE KENNEDY: Your assumption is that you must fight a war. That is wrong. We don't.

CHURCHILL: If the Germans only seek peace, surely, they won't mind if we mine the harbors of Norway.

(Joe Kennedy looks at Chamberlain.)

CHAMBERLAIN: Winston has a most secret plan to cut off Germany's supply of iron ore. If they have no iron, they can make no steel-- no steel, no tanks or airplanes.

JOE KENNEDY: That would be an act of war.

CHAMBERLAIN: Yes, it would.

CHURCHILL: Why should they care? Being the peace-loving people that they are, the Germans will have no need of iron ore.

HALIFAX: That would get the guns blazing.

CHURCHILL: Why don't you ask President Roosevelt's opinion of that, Joe? Ask what he would think if we mined the harbors of Norway to keep the Germans from their supply of iron.

JOE KENNEDY: I imagine his answer should be kept top secret.

CHURCHILL: Indeed, it should. If we could mine the harbors of Norway, we would have a distinct first mover advantage.

JOE KENNEDY: I agree with Lord Halifax. Mining the harbors would prompt a war in the west.

CHURCHILL: If the Germans found out we were even considering mining the Norwegian ports, they might attack Norway. They would be blamed for starting the war.

JOE KENNEDY: Let's not only be concerned about blame. Are you all agreed that you should prompt the Germans out of their phony war and into a very real war?

CHAMBERLAIN: No, we are not agreed on that.

JOE KENNEDY: I will ask President Roosevelt and I will make my reply only to the Prime Minister. I want no part in starting a war.

Scene 4

Jay Pierrepont Moffat sits in his office at the State Department. HIs secretary ushers in Ambassador Kennedy in December 1938.

MOFFAT: Joe, I'm so happy you could make time for a visit.

JOE KENNEDY: Thank you, Jay. I visited with the President this morning and he suggested that I follow protocol and make the rounds over here.

MOFFAT: How does the President look?

JOE KENNEDY: He's giving me the first meeting in the morning and the last meeting of the afternoon; so, I'm getting the royal treatment and I am certainly enjoying it. Seeing him first thing this morning made me realize he has aged dramatically in his job. I don't know how good his health really is.

MOFFAT: I saw in the papers that you had endorsed him for another term.

JOE KENNEDY: Of course, I want to see him re-elected, but he told me that he wouldn't run again unless we got pulled into the war.

MOFFAT: He said that?

JOE KENNEDY: That's exactly what he said. Then he said that even if there is a European war, he will not send an army over there. He said he would only commit to providing material support.

MOFFAT: Does Churchill favor expanding the war?

JOE KENNEDY: There is no doubt about that. Churchill is disappointed the Germans have not attacked London yet. He thinks of ways to induce them to attack.

MOFFAT: Why would he want London attacked?

JOE KENNEDY: If he can get the Germans to attack London, he believes Americans will feel sympathy toward the British.

MOFFAT: Well, if the Germans were abusing an Irish minority, wouldn't you want to mobilize whatever support you could against Germany?

JOE KENNEDY: I don't dispute that there is some bad blood between the Germans and the Jews. The Nazis blame the Jews for bringing America into the last war.

MOFFAT: The Jews didn't bring us into the last war.

JOE KENNEDY: There was secret agreement between the Zionists and the British.

MOFFAT: That's all unproved.

JOE KENNEDY: It is unproved for us and it is unproved for the Jews, but it is not unproved for the Nazis. A Zionist lawyer in London wrote that he thought that the anti-Semitism in Germany was directly related to that deal. That only makes it more important that we figure out a way to help the Jews get out of Germany, and now Poland.

MOFFAT: Why is that our problem?

JOE KENNEDY: It is the key to the entire conflict. I argued this last year when I proposed the so-called Kennedy Plan: if we can help the Jews get out of Germany, it will reduce the pressure on the English to attack the Germans. You're right. There are forces on Chamberlain to expand the current war-- a war which has been declared but not yet started.

MOFFAT: You're not popular in the press here, Joe, and your opinions can't be helping you in England either.

JOE KENNEDY: I'm afraid I'm done there as well. I've had good support and good press up to now, but when I've argued that the British could be overpowered by the Germans, I've been regarded as a pessimist-- a defeatist.

MOFFAT: If we entered the war---

JOE KENNEDY: ---if we entered the war, things might be different, but we don't have a modern army either. Where will the Germans be by the time we are prepared to enter the war?

MOFFAT: That seems a little harsh, Joe. You are saying that the Germans would defeat the French and the British.

JOE KENNEDY: That's what I'm saying. With Russia out of the fight, I can't see a way that they will lose. At present, Hitler has a treaty with Stalin. Germany won't lose a war with a single front.

MOFFAT: The British are going to throw you out of there.

JOE KENNEDY: I'm afraid you are right, but I've only done what President Roosevelt asked me to do and that was to tell them-- unequivocally-- that they were on their own.

MOFFAT: Things can change, Joe.

JOE KENNEDY: I know they can. I could get fired at any minute, but the President told me as recently as this morning that he would never-- repeat, never-- send an army to a European war. He did equivocate on the question of supplies and armaments, but he confirmed just two hours ago that he did not want to enter another European war. Should I be telling the British that if they get in trouble, we will bail them out?

MOFFAT: No. I'm not saying that.

JOE KENNEDY: I'm in a tough spot, Jay. I think you can see it. As I point out the obvious, the British press comes after me and the press here will soon follow suit, but I am following the instructions of my commander-in-chief.

MOFFAT: Maybe you should try to convince the Jewish leadership that you are right and they are wrong.

JOE KENNEDY: I can't understand why they don't agree with me. Of course, they are not a monolithic block and many do agree with me. I hate to see one group of Jews endanger a different group.

MOFFAT: Your concerns are very real. You are saying that war might lead to a disaster for the European Jews.

JOE KENNEDY: Hitler has said as much.

MOFFAT: The English Jews continue to resist negotiations.

JOE KENNEDY: They are not the only ones and they don't all agree; but very prominent Jewish leaders in England and in America are against taking the obvious peace agreement that Hitler has offered. I can't understand it.

Scene 5

Neville Chamberlain meets with Winston Churchill in the Prime Minister's office in January 1940.

CHURCHILL: Sources from Poland report that the Germans emptied out hospital wards for the mentally ill and turned them into barracks for their soldiers.

CHAMBERLAIN: What did they do with the patients?

CHURCHILL: The mentally ill patients were taken to nearby forests and executed.

CHAMBERLAIN: Unspeakable.

CHURCHILL: There is no depravity they will forego.

CHAMBERLAIN: Are our air forces now up to theirs?

CHURCHILL: No, we have not yet reached parity, but things are much improved.

CHAMBERLAIN: If it came to a bombing campaign, would London be hit?

CHURCHILL: Presumably they would not attack London unless we attacked Berlin. I'm sure they will avoid population centers to the extent that we avoid population centers.

CHAMBERLAIN: The same will be true of gas.

CHURCHILL: Yes. I'm sure they won't drop gas unless we do, but they have not observed any rules of warfare in Poland. It looks like it will be a brutal war.

CHAMBERLAIN: There is still time, Winston. The Germans could push Hitler out of office and we could make a peace.

CHURCHILL: We know that certain members of his army are considering just that.

HALIFAX: Is there anything we might do to help them?

CHURCHILL: I'm afraid anything we might do will result only in losing the officers trying to help us. They have enough guns to get rid of him; what they need is the opportunity.

CHAMBERLAIN: That raises the question of whether Joe Kennedy is right. Should we make a peace with a horrible man because he is the only man we can make peace with?

CHURCHILL: You've said yourself, Neville, that we cannot make peace with someone who has demonstrated such a disregard for law and rules.

HALIFAX: If you were a Jew in Poland or Germany right now, would you want us to attack or come to some agreement?

CHURCHILL: The Jews of England reject negotiations with the Nazis. The Jews of Poland might see their interests differently. We represent the Jews of England.

Scene 6

Under Secretary of State Sumner Welles and Ambassador Joseph Kennedy are received by Prime Minister Neville Chamberlain in March 1940.

WELLS: The President and Secretary of State Hull sent me to see if peace if possible. As you know, I've been in Berlin, Rome, and Paris in the last ten days and now I'm finishing up here in London.

CHAMBERLAIN: What have you found? Is there a way to avoid another full-on European war?

WELLS: Great Britain and France declared war on Germany six months ago but all parties have shown great restraint up to now. If we can find a way to de-escalate the hostilities, all of Europe might be spared.

CHAMBERLAIN: As you know, I came into this office with the declared goal of avoiding another war with Germany.

WELLS: I realize that, but now the circumstances are vastly different. Do you see any way to make a peace today?

CHAMBERLAIN: Yes, we do. If the Germans would agree to have Chancellor Hitler remove himself from power, we would agree to preserve the peace.

WELLS: You would agree to allow the Germans to keep control of the Polish Corridor?

CHAMBERLAIN: We see that as something that could be worked out over time by the Germans and the Poles. We will not negotiate with leaders who violate the rights of their own citizens based on religion.

WELLS: You will not have discussions with Hitler because he has mistreated the German Jews.

CHAMBERLAIN: That's right.

WELLS: The President is interested in restoring the peace. It might be that if we could extend the transfer agreement, we could decompress the situation. Would you be willing to negotiate with Hitler on this point?

CHAMBERLAIN: Keep in mind that I serve at the pleasure of my party and the King. While I would like to preserve the peace, and agree with Joe that any peace is better than a war, powerful forces are pushing for a showdown with the Germans. They will support leaders who are ready to make war.

WELLS: If they want a showdown with the Germans, they are going to get their wish. One of the reasons I am here is to make sure that your government understands that the United States will not be able to join you in a war against the Germans. Sentiment in the United States simply doesn't support a war.

CHAMBERLAIN: Naturally, we would hope that we could count on American support.

WELLS: I understand, but the reality is that Americans do not favor another war.

JOE KENNEDY: There is still a chance that the Germans will overthrow Hitler.

WELLS: There is a chance, but I was there just last week and I want to tell you that it is a very small chance. The Nazis have complete control of Germany and no elections are even discussed there.

CHAMBERLAIN: If His Majesty's Government deployed troops to France and the Germans attacked us there, do you believe that American sentiment would favor our cause?

WELLS: Mr. Prime Minister, Americans do not favor involvement in another European war. I can't be clearer than that. Ambassador Kennedy believes that Hitler possesses a very powerful military force which might overrun France in less than a year.

CHAMBERLAIN: We disagree.

WELLS: I understand, but if the Germans did overrun France and they remain allied with the Russians, it is very difficult to see how they could be dislodged. The Italians do not support the German anti-Semitism, but they continue to reject the forces for Communism. If all of Europe is either allied with or controlled by Germany, how could England prevail?

CHAMBERLAIN: Winston believes that cutting the Germans off from the supply of iron ore would keep them from making more weapons.

WELLS: That is true but it would also be an act of war, a provocation which the Germans would almost certainly answer.

171

CHAMBERLAIN: If we could successfully mine the harbors, Germany would not be able to make more airplanes or tanks.

WELLS: That's right. The British mined the same harbors in the last war, so the Germans are anticipating that act: Hitler would probably move against Norway if he knew you were even considering mining the harbors.

CHAMBERLAIN: Churchill has argued that such an operation might "succeed in provoking Germany into an imprudent action." He considers it "minor and innocent."

WELLS: President Roosevelt has sympathy for your efforts against the Germans, but he wants you to know that America is home to German immigrants as much as to immigrants from England. The forces for neutrality in the United States are strong. Americans do not wish to fight another European war.

Scene 7

Ambassador Joseph Kennedy speaks to Prime Minister Chamberlain on 8 May 1940 at 10 Downing Street as Chamberlain plans to resign.

JOE KENNEDY: History moves fast.

CHAMBERLAIN: It does indeed, but I ordered the harbors be mined. I had no idea how quickly the Germans would be in Norway.

JOE KENNEDY: The whole Norwegian plan was Churchill's idea. He conceived it, he planned it, he administered it, and now it has blown up in our faces and he will benefit from it.

CHAMBERLAIN: Thank goodness, we were not fighting for this island. It was a military warm up but it was a bad military warm up and I must accept responsibility and resign.

JOE KENNEDY: You tried hard to preserve the peace. Leaders have done worse.

CHAMBERLAIN: In the end, I ordered the mining of Narvik. The real war has now started, and I fear that we are not as prepared as we should be.

JOE KENNEDY: You are much better prepared than you were in Munich.

CHAMBERLAIN: Even as we re-armed, we should have pressed the Poles to come to an agreement with the Germans. It is hard to believe that an entire war will soon be fought in France and England, maybe even in other countries, over the question of Danzig. Absolute madness.

JOE KENNEDY: We both know that the war is being fought over Hitler's anti-Semitism. If the Nazis were not mistreating their Jews, there would not be the insistence that Hitler leave office.

CHAMBERLAIN: We can make no peace with such a man.

JOE KENNEDY: Countless lives will be lost if we do not.

CHAMBERLAIN: Hopefully, the French will hold their defensive line and we will be able to use the expeditionary force to push the Germans back.

JOE KENNEDY: Let's hope so. I will place a call to President Roosevelt in a few minutes to alert him that the government here will change soon.

CHAMBERLAIN: I don't know that the United States is any better prepared for war than we are.

JOE KENNEDY: Neville, let's hope for a good outcome. I'm sure the President would want me to extend his hopes and best wishes.

Scene 8

Prime Minister Winston Churchill sits with his War Cabinet on 27 May 1940. Lord Halifax and Neville Chamberlain argue across a table with Churchill.

CHAMBERLAIN: This is unprecedented in all of history. The BEF has been trapped at Dunkirk. We have no way to support them and they must either surrender or be destroyed. At this moment, Hitler calls a halt to the advance of his tanks. It is a gesture of mercy the likes of which has never been seen before in the annals of war.

HALIFAX: Hitler has promised that he has no designs on England or France. He has said that he only wishes to run Germany and leave us and the French to run our respective empires. Now he proves it to us by calling a halt to the advance of his armored column. He is trying to induce us to accept a peace.

CHURCHILL: Maybe his panzers need to be serviced. They have certainly traveled over a lot of country in the last six weeks.

CHAMBERLAIN: The Germans overwhelmed Belgium and Holland in a matter of days. France has essentially fallen in less than a month. Hitler is appealing to our sense of humanity.

HALIFAX: Unprecedented in European history.

CHAMBERLAIN: He doesn't obliterate the Tommies. He stops his armor and allows us to evacuate troops. There can be only one explanation.

CHURCHILL: What is that?

CHAMBERLAIN: Hitler knows we are in discussions about making a peace and he knows such a gesture should be taken as a sign of his sincerity.

HALIFAX: The Germans have destroyed every force put in their way in the last year and now they have the entire BEF trapped against the channel. Can you really believe he is stopping his tanks to grease the bearings? The halt order was a sign of friendship, an olive branch to us to stop the war.

CHURCHILL: How many have we gotten out?

CHAMBERLAIN: The transports, large and small, have evacuated almost 350,000 men. The Germans have not mowed down the men or sunk the rescuers.

HALIFAX: It is an act of monumental restraint. We must give him credit for this remarkable gesture.

CHURCHILL: There will be no parlay and there will be no peace.

CHAMBERLAIN: The French are using Mussolini as a conduit. They will obtain the best terms which are available and avoid further slaughter.

HALIFAX: We should at least inquire as to what form a peace treaty might take.

CHURCHILL: Making a peace now would leave Britain and her Empire at the complete mercy of the Germans. We might lose our colonies around the world.

CHAMBERLAIN: Peoples around the world are not asking for our supervision, Winston. People want to rule themselves.

HALIFAX: Peoples of other nations deserve their freedom and Hitler does not wish to occupy all of Europe. He wants independence and respect for a united Germany and he wants to leave us and the French alone. What are we fighting for?

CHURCHILL: We are fighting for the honor of our nation.

CHAMBERLAIN: Isn't it more honorable to avoid the bloodbath that a war will bring?

CHURCHILL: The British Empire will not be surrendered on my watch.

HALIFAX: The British Empire will be destroyed by the war itself.

CHURCHILL: We have recently looked at our prospects for victory. If the Navy can keep the Germans from invading England, we have two tools for victory.

CHAMBERLAIN: What are those tools?

CHURCHILL: We will defeat them by cutting off their food supplies with our blockade.

HALIFAX: Starvation.

CHURCHILL: It may not be the most humane of strategies, but it is very effective.

CHAMBERLAIN: German women and children, the noncombatants, the pacifists, the Jews, would all starve before the men who have brought this conflict to Germany.

CHURCHILL: Our second tool is long range, high altitude bombing. We will destroy German cities and demoralize her people until the leadership is overthrown.

HALIFAX: Our policy will be to drop bombs and fire on civilian populations?

CHAMBERLAIN: We have bombed German cities every night since you assumed control of the government.

CHURCHILL: Their wickedness must be stopped.

CHAMBERLAIN: Their wickedness? How would you describe a strategic plan of starving and bombing civilian populations?

HALIFAX: I will resign my position in this cabinet.

CHURCHILL: No, you will not. You are needed by your country.

HALIFAX: How can I serve a government that pretends to want peace but which rejects explicit peace offers? Hitler offered peace fully six months ago.

CHAMBERLAIN: I should have accepted the offer and aggressively re-armed England.

HALIFAX: Historians will see that Hitler offered a peace in October and he has asked for an agreement at every juncture since that time.

CHURCHILL: We cannot trust what he offers.

CHAMBERLAIN: How do we know that? Isn't that just the slogan of those who demand war? What risk do we take by allowing a peace? Can it be worse than the war we have now?

CHURCHILL: We cannot make peace with a dictator who suppresses citizens of his own state.

HALIFAX: We should wonder if we are acting in the best interests of those trapped in Germany and Poland.

CHAMBERLAIN: Your policy of starvation by blockade will not be evenly shared in Germany.

HALIFAX: Not during this war, and if we turn to anonymous killing from the skies, incineration from above, how can we expect the Germans to react?

CHURCHILL: If he invades this island, we will transfer the government to Canada and we will continue the fight.

CHAMBERLAIN: Hitler calls for peace. He issues a halt command and we answer by threatening widespread starvation and then bombing civilian centers in Germany.

HALIFAX: May the good Lord have mercy upon us.

Scene 9

Bombs fall on London in September 1940 as Ambassador Kennedy enters a war bunker to bid farewell to Prime Minister Winston Churchill. Churchill greets him holding a glass of whiskey and smoking a cigar.

CHURCHILL: They told me that you were living out in Windsor. Did you just come in for the fires?

JOE KENNEDY: No, I've been living in London and going out to Windsor only on the weekends. I'm afraid I don't get a very good press anymore.

CHURCHILL: I couldn't understand why the Germans didn't bomb London earlier.

JOE KENNEDY: Yes. You've been bombing their cities for the last 4 months.

CHURCHILL: We started the day I took charge.

JOE KENNEDY: I don't know why they've waited. Maybe Hitler held out the hope that peace was still possible.

CHURCHILL: It is not possible now.

JOE KENNEDY: That's right. It's not possible here-- not now. Of course, peace always comes. It is only a question of when and at what cost.

CHURCHILL: We're not going to make peace until we've killed him, or, until he kills me.

JOE KENNEDY: I'm glad you got your destroyers, you know.

CHURCHILL: My understanding was that you were against the deal.

JOE KENNEDY: I've been against the war-- I think everyone knows that and I can't see any possible way that Britain will be able to win.

CHURCHILL: You weren't here during the last war.

JOE KENNEDY: No, I wasn't.

CHURCHILL: I couldn't find anyone who could tell me how we were going to win the last war until, after four years of winning battles, the Germans just quit.

JOE KENNEDY: They're not going to quit this time-- not based on Wilson's 14 points. We fooled them once.

CHURCHILL: The generals might still get to Hitler.

JOE KENNEDY: If Hitler consolidates his power in France-- gets those Frenchmen to make guns for him-- and uses his U boats to keep food from getting to England, it is hard to see how you can win. Of course, I hope you do, but you're putting the future of England at grave risk.

CHURCHILL: That's the reason why having these bombs drop on London is a blessing for us.

JOE KENNEDY: Do you believe it will raise American sympathies?

CHURCHILL: Exactly. Americans will realize the justice of our cause and be moved by our sacrifice.

JOE KENNEDY: It's very graphic. President Roosevelt keeps saying he won't enter the war unless America is attacked.

CHURCHILL: He will soon see, as you will, that the best strategy for America is to have us fly your planes and drop your bombs. That keeps the war away from your shores.

JOE KENNEDY: War has a life of its own. I say that they are easy to start and near impossible to end and the loss of life always outweighs the victory.

(A bomb lands close to the bunker.)

CHURCHILL: (laughs) You know that you are always welcome to visit me here. I appreciate your positions, even if they conflict with my own-- especially if they conflict with my own.

JOE KENNEDY: I know I am. We want the same thing-- no doubt about that-- but we just disagree about how to get it.

CHURCHILL: Evil has a life of its own.

JOE KENNEDY: And war is the ultimate evil.

CHURCHILL: When do you leave?

JOE KENNEDY: In another week or so. I'm going to go say goodbye to Neville.

CHURCHILL: I'm sorry about Neville.

JOE KENNEDY: He is fine man. Must be haunting to him to think he will never know how this fight will end.

Churchill and Kennedy shake hands.

CHURCHILL: We'll never know until we arrive there.

JOE KENNEDY: It all ends somewhere, I'm sure of that.

CHURCHILL: (raises a glass to Kennedy) To old men who struggle to serve their countries.

JOE KENNEDY: (leaving) Hear, hear.

Scene 10

Former Ambassador Joseph Kennedy reads in a hospital waiting area at the George Washington Hospital in November 1941 when Secretary of the Treasury Henry Morgenthau, Jr. approaches with two security men.

MORGENTHAU: Joe?

(Kennedy looks up from his reading and then stands to greet Morgenthau.)

JOE KENNEDY: Henry-- what a surprise.

MORGENTHAU: I heard about Rosemary's operation and I wanted to come over to see you.

JOE KENNEDY: That's very decent of you, Henry. My wife is in Florida. I'm the only one here.

MORGENTHAU: I guess I knew that your daughter was having some problems.

JOE KENNEDY: Well, she has been. We thought that she might just have a difficult life but then things started to get worse.

MORGENTHAU: I'm sorry to hear that.

JOE KENNEDY: These are the best surgeons in the world.

MORGENTHAU: That's what I've heard. I had no idea there was an operation for her condition but then I read about their program here at George Washington.

JOE KENNEDY: There is a 63% chance that she will have sustained improvement. And about a 15% chance that she will stay the same.

MORGENTHAU: That's not too bad. Do you mind if I sit with you for a few minutes?

JOE KENNEDY: Not at all. I'm glad you can spare the time.

MORGENTHAU: The President knows you're over here, as well. He sends his best wishes.

JOE KENNEDY: That's very kind.

MORGENTHAU: I understand that your boys have entered military service.

JOE KENNEDY: That's right. Joe is going into the Air Corps. They are keeping his place at the law school for him while he does his service and my son Jack is looking to serve as well.

MORGENTHAU: Is he the one who is on the thin side?

JOE KENNEDY: Yes, he's got some health issues and he'll struggle to pass the physical exam, but I'm hoping he'll be able to serve in the Navy-- maybe in the Intelligence Service.

MORGENTHAU: Those are important jobs.

JOE KENNEDY: It's still not clear to me whether we'll send troops over there.

MORGENTHAU: I never thought that the United States would still be at peace in November 1941.

JOE KENNEDY: Who would have ever thought Hitler would have been stupid enough to attack Russia?

MORGENTHAU: Good for us that he did.

JOE KENNEDY: Great for us. I'm not sure I like the idea of saving the Communists in Russia.

MORGENTHAU: I understand that the Germans got caught by an early winter in Russia. Their tanks got frozen in the mud when they were a day away from Moscow.

JOE KENNEDY: That opens the door for us. If we can use the winter to get some tanks and trucks to Russia, I think I can see a way to win this thing.

MORGENTHAU: That's a new opinion for you, isn't it, Joe?

JOE KENNEDY: Not at all. I was against trying to solve the problems with a war—that's for sure—but now that we're in one, we better win it.

MORGENTHAU: It could get worse before it gets better.

JOE KENNEDY: I'm sure it will, but if we supply the Russians the way we've been supplying the British, I think it is only a matter of time.

MORGENTHAU: We'll reduce Germany to a cow pasture. We'll exterminate them.

JOE KENNEDY: I'm not in favor of that. I don't like to hear such things.

MORGENTHAU: After everything they have done?

JOE KENNEDY: Last summer I read about a fellow named Theodore Kaufman up in New Jersey. Do you know about this man?

MORGENTHAU: He's working on his own.

JOE KENNEDY: He published a book called "Germany Must Perish" in which he says that after the war, all the Germans should be castrated.

MORGENTHAU: There have been atrocities against Jews. There are probably 8 or 10 million Jews in lands under Hitler's control.

JOE KENNEDY: All the more important to talk to the Germans. Kaufman says that they are an evil people; thinks that they should be exterminated as a race.   It's dangerous to use that kind of language.

MORGENTHAU: People are angry.

JOE KENNEDY: I just question the sanity of threatening the Germans with extermination.   I heard that Goebbels had 5 million copies of Kaufman's book printed in Germany. The book shows a map of how Germany will cease to exist after the war.

MORGENTHAU: Germany should be divided among surrounding countries.

JOE KENNEDY: Henry, I just don't like it. What terrors might such threats prompt?

MORGENTHAU: We're dealing with a terrible people.

JOE KENNEDY: To propose that this is a racial war-- the idea that we would seek to eliminate all the German people because they are Germans-- is outrageous.

MORGENTHAU: We've got to beat them first.

JOE KENNEDY: It is a horrible thing, isn't it? Even when we can see some hope to win a war, it amounts to unspeakable horrors.

MORGENTHAU: Joe, I hope this operation works out for your daughter.

JOE KENNEDY: I do, too, Henry. But there are risks involved.

MORGENTHAU: Yes, I can imagine. Even if we think we are doing the right things, we must remember that there are always risks.

JOE KENNEDY: Must hope for the best.

MORGENTHAU: That's right. We hope for the best.

Two of J. A. Jensen's great uncles served with the Allies in France during World War I and other relatives served in World War II.

Interview with the author

Q: Americans generally don't believe the United States made a decision to enter World War II. Didn't it start when the Japanese bombed us at Pearl Harbor?

A: That's when the United States was attacked and formally entered the war; but in December 1941, the United States was supplying the British and the Russians with armaments to use against Germany. So, we had already taken sides in the war in Europe.

Q: The Germans declared war on us. You make it sound like the United States might have maintained neutrality in World War II.

A: Yes, that's the view expressed by the play. This play asks the question of whether the events in Europe might have been handled differently. Might we have made different choices which could have resulted in a better outcome?

Q: I've always been taught that we should have entered the second world war earlier-- we might have prevented the Jewish Holocaust if we'd attacked the Nazis. Do you disagree with that opinion?

A: Yes, I do. I am concerned that we mishandled the Nazi threat. If we had handled the threat differently, we might have avoided millions of deaths and the Jewish Holocaust.

Q: Isn't that anti-Semitic?

A: I don't believe that considering ways that the Jewish Holocaust might have been avoided is an anti-Semitic exercise. Quite the opposite: if a political arrangement might have been forged which allowed Jews to emigrate or otherwise decompressed the situation in Germany, the war might have been prevented. That was the goal of the so-called Kennedy Plan.

Q: You're making it sound like the Germans were a reasonable people. Don't you agree that Hitler had to be stopped?

A: Hitler had to be stopped at some point; we agree on that. The question is whether our policy of economic boycott, avoiding negotiations, and supplying Germany's enemies was a successful policy.

Q: We won the war.

A: Right, but we won the war at an incredible human cost. Might we have handled the situation differently, succeeded with a different political solution, and avoided 60 million human deaths?

Q: The whole premise of your play and of your unusual opinions is that it was possible to negotiate with Hitler. What evidence do you have that any reasonable government could have negotiated with Hitler?

A: I agree that my opinions are not commonly held. We agree on that point. Why do I believe it might have been possible to negotiate with Hitler? Well, I'd have to point to the historical record-- that is the entire premise of this play. Most Americans have no understanding of the events which led up to World War II.

I don't remember ever having a serious discussion about whether it was possible to make a peace after Dunkirk.

Q: What accounts for that? Why haven't we discussed Dunkirk?

A: I believe that war necessarily forces political and historical judgments to the extremes. The American response to the attack on Pearl Harbor was to mobilize for a full war. Strategies were devised to not only defend America from Japanese attack, but also to vilify the Japanese people. Japanese Americans, people who had no part in the planning or attack on Pearl Harbor, were forced to sell their hard-earned property and relocate to internment camps.

Q: How can you say our treatment of the Japanese had any relationship with what happened in Europe?

A: It only illustrates that in times of war, societies become radicalized. To mobilize an army to attack foreign peoples, the political system must convince the citizenry that there is no alternative. We must be convinced that dropping bombs on other people's homes and children is required by their animalistic behaviors and their aggressions. Part of the process is to demonize the perceived enemy. When American soldiers are returned either dead or mutilated by the fighting, the deep sadness is transformed into anger and resolution that the enemy deserves annihilation.

Q: Do you believe war polarizes public opinion?

A: Absolutely. People are asked to kill other human beings and take the risk that they themselves will be killed or maimed. Therefore, opinion must be resolute. I'm arguing that this necessity to present the case for war outlives the conflict itself, colors the discussion, and writes the history that follows.

197

Q: After the conflict has ended, it takes time to make historical judgments.

A: I agree. Can you imagine having a son or husband killed or disabled in the second world war and then read an editorial or article that argues that the war was unnecessary? Such opinions were considered treasonous during the war and for many years afterword. Some may consider such opinions treasonous even today, but it's important to scrutinize whether the right lessons of history have been learned.

Q: What about the people who lost family members in concentration camps?

A: Yes, the horrible tragedy of losing family members in a war underscores why it is so important to use the power of historical analysis to examine whether the war might have been avoided.

Q: Should we have appeased Hitler at Munich? I've never heard anyone argue that would have been a good idea.

A: In the case of Munich, the British were completely unprepared to confront the Nazis with military force and the United States was not a party to the Munich Agreement. However, the case can be made that the Munich agreement didn't go far enough: if Chamberlain had pushed for resolution of Danzig and the Polish corridor at Munich, the whole war might have been averted.

Q: We know Hitler was intent on killing the Jews. Isn't that the real reason peace was impossible with the Nazis?

A: I disagree with that position. I don't believe he was initially intent on killing the Jews-- that came later. I believe that initially he was only intent on restoring the German nation. That's what he promised his constituents.

Q: Then why did he persecute the Jews?

A: There is an enormous literature which looks at that question and so we must acknowledge that there is no one correct answer. If we read what Hitler said, we learn that he believed that the Jews were disloyal to the German nation during the Great War. That's what he wrote. His answer to that perceived disloyalty was to urge that they be pushed out of Germany.

Q: Did he believe that all the Jews in Germany should be punished for the what he thought were the political disloyalties of a few?

A: That's my understanding, but he did not initially urge genocide.

Q: What led to the genocide?

A: Again, there isn't a single answer to that question. There are many opinions. I am concerned that supporting armed conflict closed the borders, eliminated the possibilities of negotiation, and further inflamed the Germans. Our policies may have contributed to the crime itself.

Q: When you say you are concerned that our actions might have contributed to the Jewish Holocaust, are you suggesting that the United States and the U.K. might bear some responsibility?

A: It's a long discussion, but yes, I wonder if the British and American response to the Nazis might have had unintended consequences.

Q: How can you possibly say that? We destroyed the Nazis.

A: That's right, but we shouldn't forget that the United States intervened in World War I just months after the Germans proposed a peace treaty in December 1916. President Wilson favored American neutrality. If we would have stayed out that war, none of the excesses of the Treaty of Versailles would have occurred. Churchill himself said that American intervention led to much of the political upheaval that followed. That intervention ended with the Germans being starved into signing the treaty. If we ignore that chapter, we can't understand why Hitler was preoccupied with the German food supply .

Q: Are you referring to his "prophecy" speech?

A: Yes. Hitler openly threatened that if Jewish financiers were successful in turning the war into another world war, it would not end with a victory for the Jews but rather with the annihilation of the Jews of Europe. He publicly stated that warning on two occasions.

Q: That assumes that the war was being pushed by Jewish financiers.

A: No, it is only to say that is what Hitler believed. He believed that Jewish influences on the British and the American governments were conspiring to starve Germany once again and Hitler considered the Communist government of Russia to be controlled by "Judeo-Bolsheviks." Hitler foresaw that the food blockade of

World War I would be resumed and augmented in the second world war with long range, high altitude, civilian bombing campaigns-- burning German families in their homes.

Q: Does that justify the Holocaust?

A: Not at all. Nothing justifies the Jewish Holocaust. The question was what factors might have led to the genocide, and my answer is that the military response to the Nazi threat might have been part of the problem.

Q: If we hadn't gone in, might he have ordered the murder of all the Jews?

A: I don't think so. I believe if a more comprehensive deal would have been made at Munich, there might have never been a war. Or if the conflict had been stopped after the invasion of Poland, far fewer people would have died. Even at Dunkirk, even after the fall of France, it might have been possible to avert the horrible loss of life which followed, including the Jewish Holocaust.

Q: Are you asserting that the worst atrocities happened after Hitler realized he was destined to lose the war?

A: The organization and implementation of the Jewish Holocaust did not start until after Hitler was fighting on two fronts and the Americans had entered the war. If Joseph Kennedy had been able to conduct negotiations with the Germans, the whole conflict might have been resolved with diplomatic tools rather than the tools of war.

Q: Wasn't Joseph Kennedy an anti-Semite?

A: He led a very public life for most of his career and was never called an anti-Semite while he was alive. He has been thoroughly smeared since his death but, again, is this smear campaign part of our post war society's condemnation of any discussion of peaceful solutions? Is it so unreasonable to consider if the war might have been avoided?

Q: I saw a movie that showed Churchill in a subway car where the British citizens practically forced him to expand the war-- common citizens wanted the war. Are you saying that didn't happen?

A: Hollywood in; Hollywood out. There is no evidence Churchill ever met with a group of concerned citizens in a subway car. That's complete fiction. It's entertaining fiction, it's well acted and filmed, and might have won awards, but it's still fiction. I'm arguing that this subject is important enough to deserve real historical analysis.

Q: But your play is also historical fiction. How do you know that Joseph Kennedy favored negotiations with the Nazis?

A: This play illustrates Joseph Kennedy's experiences in London prior to American entry into the World War II. It is strongly based on the existing historical record and I am unaware of any material distortion of history. Like other pieces of historical fiction, it is intended to stimulate discussion and further historical scrutiny. We can't learn the lessons of history if we are afraid to consider all the evidence and competing points of view.

Made in the USA
San Bernardino, CA
17 June 2019